SALTWATER SOULS

ALSO BY HANNAH CARTER

The Depths of Atlantis (SnowRidge Press)

A Twist of Tides (SnowRidge Press)

Tide & Scale (Quill & Flame Publishing)

The Never Tales: Volume One (Twenty Hills Publishing)

The Never Tales: Volume Two (Twenty Hills Publishing)

HANNAH CARTER

SALTWATER SOULS

CONTENT WARNING:

La Llorona brings to life the Mexican folklore story and has mentions of murder, including flashbacks and some bloody scenes, but nothing overly graphic. Other stories may include sad/contemplative themes, mental health issues, or mentions of death, but all with a thread of hope throughout.

"Water is in your soul."

-Hannah Carter

PRAISE FOR SALTWATER SOULS

"A collection that will break your heart and simultaneously piece it back together while healing scars it didn't leave, *Saltwater Souls* is a book readers need. Each piece centering on every person's power of choices, Hannah Carter reminds us all that our humanity and love are beacons that we can always choose to keep shining—no matter how dark the world around us becomes. Like the sea will meet the shoreline always, let these beautiful stories remind you that there is hope always."

- Kayla E. Green, Author of *Aivan: The One Truth*

"Hannah Carter's signature blend of heartache, humor, and humanity shines through in this collection of hopeful tales that highlight the beauty and magic of connection and sacrificial love."

- Rachel Lawrence, Author of *Seashells & Other Souvenirs*

"Saltwater Souls is a collection of stories so rich that the worlds and characters contained within all feel like complete novels. Love, laughter, longing, and more lurk between these pages, and I thoroughly enjoyed every moment of it!"

- Brianna Tibbetts, Author of *Head Over Tails*

"Both haunting and hopeful, Saltwater Souls delivers an intriguing read. Carter's evocative prose sings in this beautiful, eclectic set of mermaid-themed stories."

- Kate Stradling, Author of *The Heir and the Spare* and *Brine and Bone*

For my Rikki, you poetic, noble, land-mermaid.
You are my kindred saltwater soul.
There's no one else I'd want to watch every episode of
H2O: Just Add Water *with. I love you.*

And also for me. You made it, girl.
Give yourself room to breathe now.

TABLE OF CONTENTS

THE LIGHTKEEPER 1

THE MERMAID HUNT 21

FINS FOR FREEDOM 35

SHARP AS A SIREN'S SONG 47

LA LLORONA 99

SALTWATER SOULS 119

ACKNOWLEDGMENTS 141

ABOUT THE AUTHOR 143

EXCERPT 145

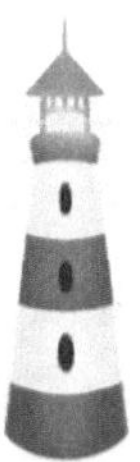

THE
LIGHTKEEPER

The lighthouse beam swept around the inky sea as Pennie stared out the window at the rain. Steam wafted up from her recently poured tea, and the faint scent of cinnamon drifted throughout the tiny sitting room of her lighthouse home.

The white curtains on the window were parted to reveal the spectacle outside; lightning illuminated the tumultuous waves and thunder rattled the house. But Pennie stayed cozy on her leather chair, a blanket bundled around her while the fire in the hearth warmed the room. Her book lay open on her lap, and the words beckoned her back into their deep world. But she could almost hear a tiny voice in her ear, like a ghost whispering beside her, *"We will stay alert and protect people, Pennie. We must be selfless during storms."*

For years, that motto had sent her into fits—especially during the worst of the hurricanes common to this area. She hated being selfless. She loathed forcing her body to stay awake when she wanted to sleep. How dare her father try to force his lifestyle on her when she simply did not fit into his world—in more ways than one. And selflessness had gotten him nothing more than a grave in Davy Jones's locker.

She swallowed a large gulp of tea, like that would somehow assuage her prickly spirit. She couldn't think that way anymore. Siren Pennie abhorred selflessness, not Human Pennie. Human Pennie wanted to be as kind and good as her father. Live up to his legacy. She valued human life and would sacrifice her own if it came down to it.

And yet, the siren inside her seethed at the very thought of giving up her wants and desires for someone else—let alone throwing away her life for them.

She tucked a strand of ashy brown hair behind a pointed ear and watched the waves outside batter the rocks. The storm was strong, but hopefully not a prelude to a hurricane. A hurricane . . . Her shoulders tensed, and, of their own volition, her eyes flicked toward the hallway and the door beyond she always kept locked. But she couldn't allow her imagination to dwell on that door, on the reminder of everything she'd lost. She flexed her toes to try to ground herself in the present and not dwell on past storms. Another sip of tea did nothing to calm her gnawing thoughts, though, so she rested the cup on the end table beside her.

It was absolutely ridiculous to be afraid of storms, because saltwater flowed through her veins on both sides of her family. Her mother's ancestors had killed unsuspecting sailors; her father's side fought to save them.

How had her mother done it? How had she overcome her full-blooded siren nature enough to love a human man and birth his mongrel child, even at the cost of her own life?

Twelve melancholic notes echoed from the grandfather clock in the front room. The lighthouse beam swept over the ocean once more.

And then she saw it.

Oh, saints below. *A ship*. A clipper with shredded sails, useless in the fight against the churning riptides. A fire blazed on the deck, spreading quickly despite the rain.

What imbecilic captain would have led his crew into such danger? Did he think he was above the ocean's fury, immune to its terrible power? Then let water fill their lungs and drown them, an adequate sacrifice for the waves—

No, *stop*. She wasn't supposed to wish for death. Shame made her cheeks flame, though no one had access to her private, wicked thoughts.

Just like the storm inside Pennie, the waters outside Stone Point Lighthouse roiled. Here, the waves lashed out unpredictably and nor'easters blew up out of nowhere to sweep sailors, no matter how skilled, away from their course. The sea loved to shatter the bones of men and boats against rocks, and the sirens rejoiced in this.

But Pennie would not.

She tossed her shawl off her shoulders and darted for the door. Wind and rain splattered against her skin, whipping her hair around her face and fighting her attempts to close the door. It took two passes of the lighthouse beacon—not to mention several swears she'd picked up from sailors—before the door latched.

"And stay there," she muttered before she turned to hasten down the cobblestone steps which led down to an old wooden dock. Out on the stormy seas, the sweep of the lighthouse beacon illuminated the narrative before her in flashes.

Several lifeboats had already left the boat, but one lingered close to the doomed ship. A man limped across the deck, another man lying limp across his shoulders. The fire lit their silhouettes as the conscious man struggled forward, almost to safety.

The conscious man latched onto a rope ladder. Descended.

The mast creaked dangerously above them.

Pennie clenched her skirt in her fist. The wind pummeled her with enough force to knock her off her feet, but she steadied herself and refused to blink. Refused to take her eyes off the men.

Die, Siren Pennie whispered.

No. Don't. Her human side felt panicked, urgently clawing at the wicked thought of the siren in her soul.

Become a sacrifice to the waves.
Stay alive.

And it was that sentiment that won out in the end. Pennie bit her lip as the siren within her sulked like a child. She could feel its rage building, its desperation to be let out. But she would keep herself contained. She conjured a picture of her father's face—his tan, weathered skin; his blue eyes and wide smile—to help her, and her breaths came more easily. When she was a child, his presence had soothed her nightmares. Now, only his presence could soothe the nightmare of her own being.

The first man stepped foot in the lifeboat, yelling. Pennie's pointed ears twitched as she focused her acute sense of hearing on their words.

"Take him! Look at his leg. Someone bandage him before he bleeds out!" the man bellowed. The sailors in the lifeboat leaped to follow his commands—he must have held power among the crew. The captain, perhaps? "Everyone's here, then?"

Pennie exhaled slowly. Everyone had survived. Everyone was on the lifeboat—

"I can't find Oliver, Captain!" another man cried. "He's supposed to be on our boat!"

The captain glanced over his shoulder to the burning ship.

"Don't you do it," Pennie warned. "Don't you go back. He could be on a different lifeboat. Don't risk your life when you may not even need to."

"I'll check," the captain yelled over the storm. "If the boat starts to sink, you go on. Don't get trapped in the undertow."

"But—"

"That's an order, Turner! From your captain." With that, the captain jumped back onto the ladder and returned to the smoke and flames of a dying ship.

Son of a *barnacle*. Did all humans have to toss their lives away so easily?

This captain reminded her so much of her father, so eager to sacrifice himself like he was nothing. Neither one of them should have ventured out in the stormy weather; it was suicidal. During that hurricane years ago, she'd begged her father not to leave, but he'd insisted. *"Lightkeepers are called to protect others. It's our job. If I don't go, Pennie, who will? You? You could. It'd be safer for you."*

He'd given her the choice. Thrown down the proverbial gauntlet for her to use her siren nature for good. But she couldn't bring herself to do it—and when it became apparent he would leave in her stead, she'd done her best to save him the only way she knew. *"Who cares about them?"* she'd yelled in all her siren fury, in all her human fear. *"It's too dangerous. They're already doomed; we shouldn't throw our lot in with them. Stop trying to be the hero. Don't go!"*

She recalled the disappointment in his eyes before he marched off to his doom and left her an orphan.

Thirteen was far too young to lose the only person she loved.

The captain had reached the top deck and disappeared. With every moment that passed and he did not reappear, Pennie took a step closer to the end of the dock. Waves crashed into the lifeboats, shoving them further off course. The sailors struggled to keep the boats steady as they waited to learn the fate of their captain and crewmate, but even all those grown men found it nigh impossible to fight the ocean's wrath.

The captain burst back into view, a young boy in his arms. Gasping, Pennie clenched her fists tighter. Sparks flew from the fire and caught onto a shredded sail. The mast groaned again, but if they hurried, they could get off the deck before the whole ship broke apart.

The captain rushed forward. Flames licked his jacket, but he had no time to stop.

"Run, you fool! Drop him and go. Save yourself!" Pennie hissed. Let the weak ones fall to the sirens below—

She growled under her breath. No. Drown those thoughts in the Great Trench. They belonged to Siren Pennie, not Human Pennie. Human Pennie wanted nothing more than for both of those men to make it out alive. And they might—they were so close, almost to the railing.

A great splintering noise rent the air.

The mast cracked.

Pennie flinched, uttering curses under her breath. Down came the mast, and the poor captain couldn't run fast enough. But right before the pole collapsed on them both, the fool tossed his companion over the railing, and the unconscious boy flopped into the water.

Heart pounding, Pennie dove into the hungry waves.

The saltwater kissed her skin and inflated her lungs as she breathed in deeply. The gills on her neck opened and fluttered, relieved to be in their natural habitat. Her legs fused into a dark salmon-colored tail speckled with yellow and stripes of purple. The colors darkened near the tips of her fins and turned completely black at the ends.

Welcome, child, she imagined the ocean whispering. *Welcome to where you belong. Among those that kill, sacrifice, serve me.*

The fabric of her skirts tangled in the fierce tide, wrapping around her. She growled and would have torn off the clothes, but she'd need them when she transformed back. As it was, she couldn't spare the minor annoyance too much thought. She had to focus on the unconscious sailor. Despite the murk and turbulence, she could make out his form—one of the few benefits of being half-siren.

Oh, Poseidon below. The closer she swam, the younger the sailor looked. He couldn't be more than eleven or so, small enough to still have cheeks rounded with youthful chubbiness.

All around her, flaming debris collapsed into the ocean, burning until the waves extinguished their eerie orange glow. Body almost vertical, Pennie stretched out her hand to the boy. A few more flicks of her tail, and . . .

She latched onto his wrist.

The water around them shuddered as the ship broke apart and sank. She swore again and barely dodged part of the mast. Curse everything and everyone—she needed to get this boy out, *now*. With a firm yank, she jerked her quarry closer to her chest and shot up through the wave, dodging planks, barrels, and other obstacles.

They broke through the surface right as lightning split the sky in half and brightened the night.

The lifeboats had gone far off course, floundering in the waves. Despite the extra hardships the crew would have as they rowed to shore, it was best to be away from anything sinking, lest they get pulled under as well. But she did have to swim farther, and by the time she got close enough to release the boy, her heartbeat and breathing rate had tripled from exertion. Perhaps a normal siren would not feel the effects of swimming, but she was a mongrel, with only enough advantages and drawbacks to be aggravating.

Once in range, she shoved the boy—Oliver, had they said?—toward a lifeboat, and hid under a torn sail. She peeked out, just enough to see everything. Oliver bobbed along the waves until someone hoisted him free. The cheers of the men drifted down to her ears, along with a cry of, "But the captain is still on the boat!"

Yes. Of course he was. Trapped under the mast of a burning, sinking ship. He'd been free, and he'd chosen to go back, to put his own life in danger.

Pennie growled. She would rescue that moronic captain just for the pleasure of drowning him herself. *After* she gave him a stern lecture about being careless and throwing his life away, of course.

Back into the cracking, smoldering debris she swam. The heat brushed against her skin as the sinking monstrosity dragged her closer to itself. She had no time to be afraid, though. Simply angry. With every plank that almost impaled her, with every smoldering net and sail that tried to entangle her, she cursed everything and everyone all to the Great Trench, right along with that captain. Would she be too late? Was the captain already dead? With every flash of lightning, white brightened the dark underworld and brought another image from her past: her father's tan and weathered face, bloated and tangled in seaweed as the ocean consumed its latest kill. The way his corpse had been *smiling*, like he was happy, even in death, knowing he'd rescued one more man.

"Stop it," Pennie chided herself as she thrust the ship's decapitated wheel away from her face. She shoved that memory back into the recesses of her brain where it belonged, where it couldn't torment her, but the past circled her mind like a shark, its teeth razor-sharp as it bit into her heart.

If she'd tried to tame Siren Pennie earlier, she wouldn't have lost her father. But her carelessness had let him perish, and now, she was the sole lightkeeper. Which meant no other human would dare throw away his life on her watch, even for the sake of others.

Not even this imbecile of a captain.

The mast hadn't released him yet. Blood tainted the water above him, but not all of his fight had faded in the minute or two he'd been underwater. He struggled, his movements sporadic and weak. Down the boat took him, straight towards Davy Jones's locker.

Thoughts wriggled into Pennie's consciousness. *The captain made this choice.*

No, *stop*. She had to keep Siren Pennie at bay.

She grabbed the mast. "It's all right. I've got you." His eyelids drooped further, and his head lolled to the side. Pennie groaned and strained to lift the broken mainmast even an inch. "Please help me," she whispered to the waves, hoping they might bend to a siren's will. She didn't know if the waves listened to her plea, but the captain slipped out from under the mast. Freed, he slumped over and floated down toward the railings.

She released her wooden burden and dodged as it sank like a large sword before following the captain into the darkness that lurked below. His eyes had drifted shut now, his whole body limp. Of course he'd gone and passed out. When had this human ever done anything remotely useful? It was up to her to do all the work, again. With a few strokes of her fluke, she latched her arms around him in a hug.

Why do you fight your nature? Her imagination conjured up the sea's taunts, ruthless and barbed. *Let him die. Sacrifice him to me and appease your nature and my hunger.*

"If you wanted me to embrace my hunger, then you never should have killed my father," Pennie snapped. "Now I'm going to make sure you never have another meal again."

So angry, the ocean taunted. *Angry at me, angry at the captain, angry at your father . . . but you know the truth. I didn't kill him. You did. You slammed your bedroom door, sulked for hours, and left him to die. You only have yourself to blame for your loneliness.*

Murderess.

Coward.

Siren.

"Go drown in the darkest pits of Hades," Pennie snarled. "You don't get to tell me what I am."

The entire exchange was quite ridiculous, to address the sea like a sentient being. But she could get mad at something with intelligence, malice. She didn't think she could handle the thought that something with neither of those qualities had stolen her father by chance, by bad luck. Her life needed a villain, and the ocean played the part so well.

She refused to lose to its waves again. She had to reach the surface before this man drowned and all her suffering was for naught.

Most of the fires had been extinguished, but that made the debris harder to evade as it broke apart and crumbled. Her skirts and the captain weighed her down, too, slowing her reaction times. One plank caught her in the head, hard enough to cause a burst of pain throughout her temple, and she swore by all the sea nymphs she knew. Her fingers brushed a charred net; she shoved it away before it could deter her anymore.

And then, blessed relief, she surfaced. The storm pounded them with sharp, chilly rain. Another wave broke over their heads and drove them under the water. But the lighthouse beacon blazed in the dark to draw her home; she focused on it as though it was a piece of golden treasure and told her aching limbs that their job was almost done.

The lifeboats were too far away—she couldn't see them at all, and the rocky shoreline was closer. She had only one option: save the captain and trust his sailors would make it to land themselves. Red rivulets of blood seeped from the captain's matted hairline to ooze across his face. He would need her medical attention—all the supplies she could offer—if he was to survive the night. Which might not have been a high priority on his list, considering his actions today, but *she'd* make sure he lived.

She would have no one to berate for his foolish actions if he didn't.

Pennie placed her hand over his forehead to protect his laceration as she guided him back to the shore. She'd snatched a meal from the ocean's hungry maw, and it tantrumed and lashed at her as punishment.

Coughing, Pennie reached the rocky coast and hauled the unconscious captain onto the rough sand. Her tail disappeared when she escaped the frothing waves, and she dragged the captain farther inland with her shaky limbs. Her skirt tangled around her legs, making the journey more arduous as she nearly tripped with every step. Curse it to both the Great Trench and Davy Jones's locker! It would take too long to reach the lighthouse if she had to fight the weather, her own clothing, *and* the unconscious captain's weight.

She lowered him onto his back, far enough away from the ocean that its angry waves couldn't hurt him. Then she turned him on his side, delivering several solid thumps to his back until he vomited up the water he'd swallowed. His body convulsed wildly as it tried to expel the foreign liquid from his lungs.

Several minutes passed until he slumped against her lap, his eyes at half-mast. ". . . Oliver?" he rasped.

"Safe." Rain lashed against Pennie, and angry tears warmed her cheeks. "You *imbecile*!" It felt good to get the words out, to unleash her pent-up anger on the unsuspecting soul who'd drawn it out of the depths.

The man's brow furrowed. ". . . What?" His eyes didn't focus on her—never even opened all the way. Blood clumped his hair together and trickled down his face.

"Oh, blast it all. I can't yell at you until you're coherent enough to understand," Pennie grumbled. Louder, she added, "You've been sliced. Can you walk?"

The captain mumbled something too slurred for her to catch.

She checked the wound and sighed. "You'll need stitches. I'll have to give them in the lighthouse. If you can stand, that would be best. I'll help steady you."

Whether it was from his head injury, near-death experience, or a general affability, the captain didn't protest as she led him to the lighthouse. With the slippery rocks around the coast and the rain beating down on her, the journey was agonizingly slow. But when she finally swung open the door to her home, the fire greeted her and melted some of the tension from her chilled bones.

"Here. Sit." She guided him to the chair she'd inhabited before this whole ordeal and placed a blanket around his shoulders.

The captain shivered, his teeth chattering. He opened his mouth, but Pennie cut him off with a fierce glower, one that would make a school marm shudder. "Don't talk just yet. It'd be just my luck for you to shiver so hard you bite your tongue off." She glanced outside her large window. "If you're going to ask about your crew, they'll be here shortly, I'm sure. I last saw them battling the waves on their way here. They'd been blown far off course, but they were safe. If you want any chance at being reunited, you'll have to cooperate and let me stitch you up." She leveled a finger at him. "Stay here while I fetch my supplies."

After tossing another log into the fire, Pennie gathered several blankets and draped them around his shoulders and legs.

There. That should help him regain some warmth in his limbs. Now, to set her sights on collecting the rest of the supplies she needed.

Within a few minutes, she'd fetched her medical kit, a basin of warm water, and some alcohol. When she returned, the captain had made himself quite at home, his shoes off and his chair closer to the hearth. His black hair hung in limp strands across his forehead. Despite the dampness, they were already fighting to curl.

The captain glanced up as she entered. "Th-thank you," he said, his voice low and tired. "You saved my life."

Pennie tied off the end of her suturing thread, positioning it on the firebox so it could warm. All the while, she tried to keep her temper from flaring like the flames. The ocean's—her own—thoughts from earlier churned inside her, mocking her. *So angry. So angry at everyone. Why are you so angry?*

Irritation bubbled up and scalded her insides, and she had to release it with harsh words before it burned her alive. "I wouldn't have had to save you if *you* wouldn't have been so eager to throw your life away."

"I could not let the lad drown. He's only ten, and besides that, it's my job to protect my crew. And Oliver . . . he looks to me as a father, of sorts. And no father would let his son perish." The captain slid off his sock and wiggled his bare foot at the fire.

Father. The word jabbed at Pennie as if she'd thrust a sewing needle into her skin. She didn't need a lecture from someone without a single gray hair on what *fatherhood* entailed.

The captain shivered as he slipped out of another wet sock. The two thoughts combined—wet socks, fathers—struck a realization inside her. "I'll go get you some dry clothes." She passed him a washcloth soaked with alcohol. "Hold this against your wound while I'm gone. It needs to be cleaned as well, lest you get a nasty infection."

He nodded, yelping as the linen touched his forehead. His whole body shuddered, and he pinched his eyes shut.

Good. The pain would keep him conscious, and new clothes would keep him from hypothermia.

Yet, to fix the latter, she'd have to do something she'd sworn to herself she'd never do. She'd have to venture into her father's room, and she'd kept the door locked ever since his death.

With every step she took through the small stone house toward her destination, sorrow seemed to follow. She wanted to snarl at it, send it back to the shadows, refuse to acknowledge it. She preferred anger; it was much easier to manage. Anger would not break her so much as her grief would.

A flash of lightning brightened the hallway, and thunder grumbled as she rested her hand on the doorknob. Even the weather seemed to protest, to insist that entering her father's room would be the cardinal sin. It would make the unfathomable heartache *tangible*. Her father would not be, his broad form standing by the window with a wide grin on his face. She would see only emptiness. Grief. Loneliness.

Blast that captain.

With a deep breath, she turned the doorknob and entered into the sacred sanctuary.

Her father hadn't made his bed on his last day, and the sheets were still rumpled. The closed door had trapped the faint traces of his cologne inside the room. Those traces clung to everything and were especially strong near the dresser, where the half-used bottle sat.

Pennie covered her mouth, her whole body trembling. The first few tears spilled over onto her cheeks; the scent of her father was so vivid that she wanted to reach out and touch him.

Lightning flashed outside the bay window. Rain slapped the glass with mad fervor as Pennie drifted toward the bed, her hand still pressed against her mouth to keep from wailing.

She'd had such terrible nightmares as a child. Some related to childhood fears, while some related to all the things her siren nature wanted her to do. But each time she'd been scared, she could come in here. Her father would wrap his warm arms around her, hold her close, and whisper stories in her ear about brave children defeating all sorts of monsters. If they could do that, she could go back to sleep and best Siren Pennie.

Her free hand drifted over the red woolen sheets. She almost gave in to the urge to fall right into bed, wrap herself up in fabric that still smelled like him, and stay there forever. But thoughts of the captain prodded at her, and she knew she could only take a minute to grieve.

So she sat on the edge of the bed and brought a sheet to her nose.

Tears trickled down her face, dripping onto the fabric. Her father's ghost may not have been *in* the room, but he certainly haunted every corner of it.

"Why did you have to leave?" she murmured. "I still needed you. I still have nightmares." Her voice broke.

Curse being half-human. Curse having *emotions*. They could join the captain in the Great Trench, then Davy Jones's locker, and then in the bowels of Poiseidon's fury.

She allowed herself a few more moments to cry in the darkness, to think about her father, until it hurt too much and her common sense told her she needed to get back to the topic at hand.

A few minutes later, she exited her bedroom, dressed in a dry outfit. Into the living room she went, where she thrust a woolen sweater, pants, and socks toward her guest. "Hurry and change in the next room so I can stitch your wound. The needle should be hot enough now."

The captain swayed as he followed her orders. While she waited, Pennie pinched the knot of the thread between two fingers and withdrew the needle, dipping it in alcohol to sanitize it. The captain emerged from her washroom soon after and slumped into a chair. He lowered the washcloth, now bloody, and examined her with tired eyes. "Thank you. For everything. Are you sure your husband won't mind me borrowing his clothes?"

"I don't have a husband. They're my father's." Pennie's voice came out sharp, and she cleared her throat so she could start over with a lighter tone. "Now hold still." She knelt in front of him. Gently, she nudged his curls away from his forehead. "This will hurt."

She pressed the needle into his skin.

The captain hissed and flinched. His grip on the chair turned white-knuckle, and the tendons on his jaw tightened until she could see them popping.

"Don't close your eyes," she chided. "It may hurt, but if you wrinkle your forehead, you'll interfere with my work. You must relax."

He gave a pained chuckle. "Something tells me you've never had a needle jabbed through your forehead."

"I am, in fact, not stupid enough to be injured when saving someone." Her siren side bristled at the idea of saving anyone, which made her own accusations from earlier flare up again. *Murderess. Coward.*

Siren. Her hand faltered, and she might have tumbled down a very long train of self-deprecating thoughts, but the captain broke the silence.

"I don't know about that." He reached up and brushed a bruise on her forehead.

Pennie twitched, more so from a reaction to being touched than pain. "That's your fault," she retorted. "I wouldn't have been hit by debris if you hadn't been on a burning ship to begin with!"

"It looks like you might have a pump knot. Shouldn't you ice it? Or . . . does your siren magic heal you?" the captain asked softly—right before he bit off a curse as she tugged the needle through his skin with more force than necessary.

"What do you know?" she demanded, eyes narrowed. Her voice might have been sharp, but most of her brusqueness came from surprise.

He chuckled weakly. "Come now. I didn't hit my head *that* hard. I saw your tail before I passed out. You're a siren."

Pennie eyed him skeptically. "You're taking the news rather well."

"A side effect of my head injury, I assure you." He sighed, his breath metered. "Besides, every sailor has a story or two about sirens. Mine will tell of the night a beautiful siren rescued me."

Her pulse rushed inside her head, and her cheeks warmed. Dratted captain. Stupidly noble *and* a charmer? He made her want to shove the needle deeper into his skin. "*No.* You can't tell anyone about me. This lighthouse . . . It may not seem like much to you, but humble as it is, it is my way of living, and I have nowhere else to go. No other family would accept a halfling such as myself."

When the captain spoke again, his voice was as low and soft as the ocean on a calm day. "I assure you, your secret is safe with me. I owe you a debt of gratitude. You saved my life."

Heat sparked in her veins and the metaphorical hackles on Siren Pennie's neck rose. Let this man be soft and warm like a gentle wave—she would be fierce and sharp like the hurricane. "Yes, I did. But I wouldn't have had to if you hadn't tried to throw away your life!"

"What—what are—" He furrowed his brow, which tugged on her string and earned him a sharp yank.

"Stay *still*. Unless you believe your stunt earlier wasn't suicidal enough and want to finish the job." Pennie tugged the stitches tighter and snipped the string. Then, perhaps a bit more angrily than she should have, she plunged the washcloth back into the alcohol and thrust it against his injury again. Siren Pennie rejoiced when the captain flinched; Human Pennie didn't have time for a reaction before she launched a verbal attack.

"You called yourself the father to that boy. Are you a father to any other children, Captain?"

His rust-colored eyes widened. "No—"

"Do you have a wife?"

"No."

"Have you *any* friends or family?"

"Yes . . ."

Pennie's nostrils flared. "Then how *dare* you act as if there is no one who will miss you if you die." The heat inside her chest flared as potently as the fire behind her. A log sparked and crackled, and a bead of sweat tickled her neck.

"I never thought of it that way." The captain's jaw tensed. "But there are people who would miss my men, too. And as a captain, I must think of them."

"So it doesn't matter if you die, as long as you get to be a hero? As long as your men go home and boast about how you gave your life to save theirs?"

"If I have to lay down my life for someone, then I will gladly do it." The captain's voice matched her fervor. "And I don't see why it's any of your business."

"Of course you don't." Pennie's breath came in ragged heaves. When she opened her mouth again, she didn't know whether it was Siren Pennie who spoke or just a heartbroken daughter. "Heroes never think of the people they leave behind. Those of us who have to suffer without them."

Silence stretched between them, broken only by the popping logs and the rain that hammered against the window. The grandfather clock chimed, and Pennie imagined soon the sailors would come for their grand, heroic captain.

He rested a gentle hand against her shoulder. "I'm sorry."

Pennie sniffled. Subtly, she daubed at her wet nose with the washcloth before she bunched it up and tossed it next to the alcohol bowl. "What's done is done."

"Spoken like someone who wishes something could be undone," the captain said. "Like you once knew a hero."

Perhaps years of loneliness had eaten away at the barriers around Pennie's heart. Perhaps she wanted to use her own story as an example. Or perhaps something in the captain's demeanor made her want to trust him, as reckless as he might be.

"My father," she whispered. "The previous lightkeeper. He tried to rescue sailors in a similar storm. He didn't survive, and I have been alone ever since."

To the captain's credit, he didn't ask why Pennie had not rescued the sailors or her father. Did not press for the details of that awful day, of how she'd locked herself in her room to pout. He didn't make Pennie relive the helplessness she'd felt as she swam for hours, trying to find where the tides had tossed her father, only to be too late to save him.

Pennie clutched fistfuls of her skirt and turned her head away from the captain's gentle gaze. "When a life for a life is exchanged, it doesn't negate the suffering." Her voice cracked. "It only changes who suffers."

"And yet, you still jumped. You came to rescue me." He squeezed her shoulder. "It sounds like your father raised a heroic daughter, too."

She snorted. "No. Merely a daughter trying to make penance for her wicked nature." Her selfishness, which had caused her father to perish when he went out instead of her. How she could never act selflessly without feeling *bothered* by it. Her temper, her spite, how she held grudges. None of those negative traits had been inherited from her father.

The captain shook his head. His grip on her shoulder grew a bit tighter, to the point she glanced up to make sure he wasn't about to pass out from blood loss. But their gazes met, and his eyes carried so much compassion she nearly lost her breath. "Don't slave your life away trying to atone for what haunts you. That will only make you miserable. You are a hero, Pennie. At least to me."

Pennie sighed. "I'm no hero." Quieter, she added, "I just miss my father."

Blast that captain *again*. Hot, furious tears spilled from her eyes. She couldn't swipe at them quickly enough—or at all when her guest slid off his seat and wrapped his arms around her. Thanks to the clothes she'd loaned him, he smelled like her father, and Pennie suddenly regretted her choices. It only made her sobs that much harder to hold in.

"I only wish that I could apologize," she choked out. "If—he could see me now. I try. I try every day to be better than the siren inside of me. To not be the monster—to be better than that, like he told me I could be. I stay here for him. So that he can know . . . he was a good father."

Outside, the lighthouse beacon continued to illuminate the night, a guide to wandering sailors everywhere and a promise that they could find warmth and safety here. And she would make sure that it always burned, just as her father would have. He had not raised Siren Pennie. He raised Human Pennie—even if Human Pennie came with a tail.

"He must have been a good man for you to love him so deeply," the captain murmured. His arms tightened around her and made her all the more cognizant of his presence. Did he have to embrace her, though? She didn't know whether to loathe or tolerate it, the first hug she'd had in . . . in a very long time. "And I know he was because he raised a kind daughter."

"If you knew inside me, the siren nature—the things I've thought—you wouldn't think so. Sirens are dangerous creatures. Selfish murderers." Pennie wormed her way out of the captain's arms. With her long sleeve, she wiped at her face, tucking a strand of long, damp hair behind her ear.

"Perhaps your experience with humans is limited, but there are selfish murderers among us, too." The captain's lips quirked. "Besides. Tonight, you saved my life *because* you're a siren. You may have more struggles because of whatever nature you fear lurks inside you, but that only makes your sacrifice all the more impressive. You have taken what you fear is monstrous and used it for good."

Hesitantly, Pennie's fingers brushed the closed gills on her neck. The very slits that helped her breathe underwater—and the reason why the captain and Oliver were still breathing, too.

She had always separated herself, considered the two parts of her soul too vastly different to ever coincide. But her parents had loved one another, no matter how short a time they'd had. Could it be that Siren Pennie and Human Pennie weren't such distinctive parts, but . . . one whole?

Not a monster. A temperamental, inherently selfish, lonely girl who had loved someone as deep as the ocean and had them snatched away. A girl who wanted to do right despite the less favorable parts of her nature.

Someone banged on the door, and Pennie started with a gasp. She grasped the captain's knee, and he rested his larger hand on hers, giving it a squeeze.

"Help! We need help! Our boat sank, our captain is missing—" a voice called over the wind.

"Louis!" The captain's eyes brightened as he lifted his voice. "Louis, it's me. Captain Brown."

"*Captain?*" Disbelief tinged the sailor's words, and he rattled the locked doorknob. "Captain, are you all right? How did you get in here?"

"I'm coming!" Captain Brown yelled. "I'm fine, Louis. The lightkeeper rescued me." He cast her a smile, and her cheeks flushed again, suddenly very aware that the captain's hand lingered on hers, which made even more heat rise to her face.

The grandfather clock ticked as their time drew to a close. Extricating herself, Pennie rose and helped Captain Brown to his feet. He had a few inches on her, and thus stared down at her. "I never did get your name," he whispered.

Her heart fluttered despite her best attempt to keep her emotions caged. "Pennie. Pennie Smith."

"Thank you, Pennie Smith. For saving me tonight." Captain Brown drew one of her hands to his lips and brushed the faintest of kisses across her knuckles, though it was enough to make her face flush.

"And your name?" she asked, if only to hide her embarrassment. "I feel it is only right to know the name of the man I saved."

"Ezra Brown."

Outside, the sailor beat against the wooden door. "*Captain Brown?*"

A crooked smile split Ezra's face. "As you can probably tell, *Captain Ezra Brown.*"

"Well. Pleased to meet you, Captain Ezra Brown." Pennie's knuckles burned where he'd kissed them, and a similar fire seared her back, where his hand rested just underneath her shoulder blades. "Now, why don't you open my door before your men beat it down? They'll need refuge from the storm."

Ezra released her and stepped toward the door. "Thank you. For everything you've done tonight for me and for my men. Next time I visit, I promise it will be on better terms." He chuckled. "No more falling overboard just to get your attention."

"See to it you don't." Pennie smiled and surprised herself by shooing him away with a teasing motion of her own. "Now, let them in. You don't want your men to catch their death of cold."

Hours later, as dawn broke, Pennie settled into bed, content, with her siren nature subdued, perhaps even happy at being appreciated. Ezra and his crew had made port, the storm had dissipated, and another night had passed without anyone—hero or otherwise—perishing in her waters.

Siren, human, or both . . . she believed her father would be proud of her tonight.

THE
MERMAID HUNT

Ross! Did you see it? Did you see the mermaid?"

Ten-year-old Evie burst onto the houseboat deck, her dark curls bouncing with each step. The door to the inside salon slammed shut behind her, rattling the windows, and Rosslyn jolted awake at the sudden noise. "What? Slow down, Evie." She rose from her seat on the lower deck, staggering for a few steps until her brain fully woke up.

"No way!" Evie's loud voice must have carried across the water to the shoreline, because the birds in the not-so-far-away trees took off into the sky, cawing their indignation.

Evie paid no attention to the happenings around her. She donned a red life jacket, incorrectly buckled; of *course* Dad had let her out of the safer, covered part of their boat without checking to make sure the life jacket was properly secured.

Indignation bubbled up inside of Ross. She hadn't asked to play babysitter, hadn't asked to be back out on the houseboat at all. But she also hadn't asked for *any* of the other crap that had happened to her throughout the last year. Yet today, like every other day, Ross's feelings were sacrificed on the altar of her father's work as an aquatic biologist, just like when her father had relocated his family right before her senior year of high school.

"Why not?" Ross asked, crossing her arms.

"I can't slow down. She might get away!" Evie's voice carried a high-pitched, excited tone, which agitated even more birds on the shoreline.

"Shh. Who might?" Ross pushed one of her messy braids, stuffed with her untamable red hair, behind her freckled shoulder. A bead of sweat trailed down her loose strapless shirt, and she shuddered as it tickled her spine.

Yet another reason to despise being out on the water today: her ginger inclination to fry in the scorching sun.

Evie rolled her eyes, answering like an exasperated parent. "The *mermaid*, Ross!"

Ross sighed. Great—yet another mermaid-related incident she'd have to report to Evie's therapist. "*Yes, she's regressing. She's still trying to convince us that mermaids are real. I think she's a maladaptive daydreamer. I've been researching it.*"

Dad said she didn't *have* to take notes. That he could handle Evie's appointments well enough. He and Ross's therapist were much more interested in figuring out why Ross, a formerly straight-A student, had barely passed her junior year. Why she suddenly had a string of detentions on her record after skipping too many classes and falling asleep during lectures. But Ross spent almost all her therapy appointments focused on Evie, to everyone's chagrin.

A boat sped by, and their vessel rocked with the waves it left in its wake. Ross hissed and snagged hold of Evie's lifejacket before the bouncy ten-year-old plummeted into the water. Ross's heart pounded, and the waves seemed to mock her.

Why don't you come in and join us, Ross? Just like your mother.

Bile churned in her stomach, and she tugged Evie away from the railing to fix the jacket. Clenching her teeth, Ross counted backward from ten, one of the many coping techniques she'd found on the internet.

See? She didn't need a therapist. She'd fallen down so many rabbit holes about trauma and childhood development that she could therapize herself *and* Evie if need be.

"That's too tight, Ross," Evie muttered as Ross cinched the life jacket over the girl's belly. "Let me go! The mermaid's getting away."

Ross pursed her lips. Time to de-escalate the mermaid situation. "We're on a lake in the middle of Florida, Evie. There are no mermaids here." She held herself back from adding, *"or at all."*

"I *saw* one." Evie pointed her finger in the general direction of the water. "I saw her surface. I really did!"

"Regardless—" Ross clicked the last life jacket clip into place. "What are you going to do, jump in after her? You can't. Haven't you heard about all the flesh-eating bacteria and stuff? Besides that, you could drown." Ross's voice hitched on the last word.

"I won't drown," Evie mumbled. She scowled at the wooden deck. "And quit trying to be the new Mom. You aren't her."

A flash of anger broke through Ross's tired façade, and she wanted to shove her sister into the water. Not so long ago, she would have done it. Now, she did her best to swallow down her irritation, but her tone still sounded clipped. "You may think you're a strong swimmer, but it doesn't matter. Even the strongest swimmer can drown."

"I won't drown," Evie repeated. "Because I'm a mermaid too."

Irritation bubbled beneath Ross's skin and made her itch. "There's no such thing as mermaids, Evie. All the reported sightings were from sailors centuries ago and were more than likely manatees or dolphins. Or even hallucinations. No telling what Molotov cocktail of diseases they had, and any one of those ailments could have made them see stuff." In lieu of throttling her sister, Ross gave Evie's shoulders three squeezes—their family signal for *"I love you"*—in an attempt to soften her next words. "Besides, even if mermaids *were* real, *you* aren't a mermaid. I would know. I've been swimming with you countless times, and not once did you sprout fins."

"Nuh-uh. I *am* a mermaid." Evie fingered the mermaid necklace their mother had gotten for her at some aquarium in Gatlinburg a few years ago. Evie never took the thing off—to the point where some of the fake diamonds were missing and the chain had rusted. "Mom said so."

Ross's heart twisted and she had to turn away before Evie could see the tears that threatened to spill over. Covering her mouth, Ross stared at the horizon, at the tall trees that reached toward the sky and cut the three of them off from civilization. Nothing but Ross, Evie, their father at the helm, and the lake below.

If Ross slipped beneath the waves, how long would it take for someone to notice? To *care*?

Oh, whatever. Ross rubbed her eyes. She didn't have enough energy to try to break through Evie's intense daydreaming. Might as well play along until Evie's therapist could get ahold of her. "Okay, fine. You're a mermaid, but you still need your life jacket on. It's against the law for little kids to be on a boat without one."

"*You're* not wearing a life jacket." Evie tilted her head. It was the way she always did things—she'd deliver a sassy remark and then "cute" her way out of it. "And I'm ten now. Double digits. So I can be just like you."

Ross sighed. "You *just* turned ten, so it barely counts. Besides, I'm seventeen. Legally, I don't have to wear a life jacket." Neither did Evie, *technically*, but Ross wasn't about to tell her that. Florida's life jacket laws were ridiculously lenient.

And the only reason you just don't want to wear one is because if you fall into the lake, you don't want anything to stop you as you go down, down, down, just like your mother, the deep and dark voice in the back of Ross's head hissed.

"Anyway, it doesn't matter," Ross muttered. She didn't know *what* she meant didn't matter, specifically—just life in general. "Why don't you go back to Dad?" At least then Evie would be *inside* the houseboat's salon and away from the water. But then she'd *also* be closer to Dad and all his ideas. He'd barely given them a solid year to mourn before he ushered them back onto the water.

"You've been raised on a boat your entire life, Ross. What do you want me to do, give up my career? Everyone in this family would die if we were land-bound. Water is in your soul, just like it's in Evie's."

Water had also been in their mom's soul.

And then her lungs.

"Ross? *Ross*, you're not listening to me." Evie grabbed Ross's hand. "I said I don't want to. I want to go on a mermaid hunt. *Please* come with me?"

Ross scratched the end of her wide, freckled nose. Maybe she could convince Evie not to go into the water by using the daydream's logic. "We can't. Mermaids are an endangered species, like the giant panda, so we can't hunt them."

Evie scowled. "You think I'm kidding."

"No—no, I don't—"

"Yes, you do. You never take me seriously." Evie's shoulders drooped as she plopped down on the edge of the houseboat. Her legs dangled in the water, and even her curls suddenly seemed less vibrant and lively.

Ross crouched next to her sister. Tangled, jumbled thoughts ran through Ross's mind, but whenever she tried to grasp one to express herself, it slipped away like it was nothing more than a cloud of smoke. "It's just—" The thought evaporated. Her tongue wasn't quick enough to claim it, and she was too exhausted to chase it. Sighing, Ross gave in fully to her sister's make-believe; it was just the easiest thing to do. "All right. I'll help you hunt mermaids. But you've got to promise me you'll keep your life jacket on. I'm sure your mermaid is too busy for an underwater rescue."

Evie squealed and clapped her hands together.

"Use the ladder and—" Before Ross could finish her instructions, Evie leaped into the water, spraying droplets everywhere. Ross grasped the boat railing as her heart stuttered in her chest and filled her stomach with nauseated butterflies. But Evie's head bobbed above the surface, and she waved up at Ross.

"Jump in! It feels great!"

Fantastic. Ross hadn't even had a chance to tell their dad they were going swimming, but did it really matter? He couldn't be bothered to pay attention to anything besides his work.

Grumbling under her breath, Ross lowered herself into the lake. The chill hit her body and made her shudder. Quickly, she dipped under the water, letting it cocoon her. Time seemed to slow around her. Her heartbeat resounded in her ears, and she let out a bubble of air.

So quiet.

So dark.

So *nice*.

She could stay here forever.

It took all her self-control to re-emerge into daylight with a gasp. She shoved some loose strands of hair away from her face, her body temperature adjusted. The lake felt nice now. Like a second habitat. Like being sandwiched between the water and the sun was right where she belonged.

Until Evie splashed Ross full in the face.

Ross sputtered, the unexpected assault robbing her of any pleasure she'd just experienced.

"Feels good, doesn't it?" Evie grinned, the gap where her incisor tooth had once been on full display. "It's because mermaids get weak when they're away from the water. We have to recharge ourselves every once in a while or we'll lose every bit of magic."

Part of Ross wanted to shake her sister, to yell at her that this was delusional, that Evie was burying her grief in this fantasy. But she swallowed her unhelpful desire and instead warned, "*Don't* splash me. I don't like it." One more deep breath and Ross was able to calmly add, "And that's . . . interesting. I never knew that."

"That's because I listened to *all* Mom's stories. She told me everything." Evie started to doggy-paddle away. "Follow me. I saw the mermaid over here."

Evie swam to an open area, an area in which the two girls were probably in danger of being run over by a jet ski or another boat. That didn't seem to deter Evie at all, though.

Ross ducked under the water to get some relief from the brutal sunshine for her shoulders and neck. As much as she hated to admit it, she *did* feel a bit better now that she was in the lake. Not that her problems seemed smaller; she simply felt more equipped to handle them.

Talk about a placebo effect at its finest. "Tell me about this mermaid, Evie. We have to be scientific about our search."

"Well, she had a pink tail. I know that much. And her hair matched, too. It was really pretty." Evie bobbed along in her little red life jacket. Sunlight glittered on the water and made a sparkling path. "Look at the sunshine, Ross! It reminds me of the magic in *The Little Mermaid* when Triton turns Ariel into a human. Don't you think so?"

Great. Evie was probably swimming straight toward the sun's reflection just so she could undergo some magical transformation.

Evie didn't wait for Ross to reply. "Do you know that when mermaids get legs, their hair changes color? When they're in water, they have the same color hair as their tail." Evie tilted her head, treading water. "And—echo—eco—what's that word for where things live?"

Ross checked for any boats, but she couldn't see or hear anything dangerous beyond the water itself. "Natural habitat? Were you trying to say ecosystem?"

Evie nodded. "Okay, that thing—well, just like how different types of fish have different natural habitats, mermaids have different types too. Some live in freshwater lakes. Some live in saltwater . . ."

This seemed to be a good time to redirect Evie's focus back to reality. "Did you know that Florida not only has freshwater lakes, like the one we're on, but saltwater ones?"

Evie huffed. "Who *cares*? You always have to prove that you're the smartest. That's why Mom never told you her stories. She knew you'd just dissect them instead of believing."

Ross stopped swimming. It would have been nicer if her sister had smacked her across the face. "Excuse me, but what?"

Evie turned around. The life jacket pressed her cheeks together and made them appear even chubbier. "You know. You and Dad always try to make things logical and factual and all that junk. You never believe. *That's* why Mom didn't tell you stories like she told me. I bet you don't even believe in mermaids. You probably just don't want me to get eaten by a shark."

You didn't deserve the stories your mom told. You didn't deserve to hold onto the scraps of memories like your sister, that dark whisper hissed. *She always liked Evie better, because all you two did was fight with each other. No wonder she didn't want to spend time with you. No wonder she was always so engrossed in her work.*

Even the cool water couldn't fix the heat that filled Ross's body. Fiery words tumbled out of her lips, and for the first time, she felt more like her old combative self, the girl who used to argue with her mother until neither of them could stand the sight of each other. "Well, excuse *me*, you little sparkly princess. I forgot you could magically protect yourself with your stupid mermaid magic. It sure worked well for Mom, didn't it, huh? When she *drowned?*" Ross's voice pitched higher and louder. The sun's unforgiving rays added to her irritability as they mercilessly burnt her back. "That's what believing in silly little fantasies gets you. A head full of dreams and lungs full of water." Not even Evie's wide eyes and open-mouthed gawk could stop Ross. She was a shark in bloodlust, shredding everything to bits around her, unwilling to stop until the water was stained red. "And *for another thing*—I *am* worried about a shark eating you! Bull sharks can live in fresh water and salt water, so—so—*there!*"

Evie's nostrils flared, just like they always did when she fought back tears. Her mouth twisted into a scowl and she splashed Ross in the face again—this time, not in good fun. "Shut up and listen to me! You're missing the whole point!"

"No, *you're* missing the whole point!" Ross's voice echoed across the water. The part of her heart that had been wounded now wielded ammunition prepared for retaliation. "You're living in some delusion that mermaids are real because you don't want to face the truth. Mom wasn't a mermaid, Evie. She was a marine biologist. She was a marine biologist who *drowned* in a tragic accident."

Evie lost the battle with her tears. They started to stream out of her dark eyes, but her voice never lost any of its fire. "You're wrong! She told me. She told me she might have to leave, but that I could find her, and—"

"She drowned and they never found her body, Evie! So *grow up* and stop daydreaming!"

Evie covered her eyes, but her shoulders shook with the force of her sobs. Ross turned away, her chest heaving. Ross may not have been anything like their mom, but Evie had inherited at least one trait—she knew how to press all of Ross's buttons.

A few yards away from the houseboat, a rocky inlet jutted out into the water. With a few big strokes, Ross reached it and climbed up. Tiny puddles had gathered on the uneven surface, and waves lapped against Ross's feet. Her little inlet, sequestered away from civilization, reminded her of *Island of the Blue Dolphins*, her favorite childhood book. She'd often fantasized about what it would be like to be abandoned on an island like the main character and have to create a life all by herself. Maybe Ross could stay out here, all alone, and no one would ever know. She had enough knowledge to survive by herself, and no one would miss her.

No one would care if she and her impetuous tongue drowned, forgotten and alone.

Evie swam over, her face red and blotchy, moisture clinging to her eyelashes. She could barely hoist herself out of the water and onto the large rocks, so Ross huffed and tugged her up. Once she was safe and sitting down, Evie picked up a few stray pebbles and tossed them into the lake, sniffling all the while.

Ross gathered her legs up to her chest and stared blankly across the shimmering expanse. She didn't have the fortitude to break the silence until five *plunks* later. "I'm sorry I yelled at you." She leaned over and wiped Evie's eyes, a small truce.

"It's okay." Evie tossed another rock in, and it sank to the bottom with a wet *thunk*. "I would be sad and angry, too, if I thought Mom had really died."

Ross let out a tired exclamation and let her forehead thump against her knees. Her thick braids swung forward and smacked her legs, and escaped tendrils of hair tickled Ross's skin. She shivered.

Evie leaned her head against Ross's arm. "Would it really be so bad if you believed in mermaids? In all Mom's stories?" Evie's voice was garbled with emotion.

"Yes, it would be. Because that would mean I was delusional. This is a process of grief. You've got your mermaids, Dad has his research to make him feel closer to her, and I've got . . ." What *did* Ross have? Oh, yes. Severe depression, a tinge of avoidance, and a lifetime's worth of arguments and regrets.

Evie might have been convinced she couldn't drown, but awake or asleep, Ross sank further beneath the water's surface, and one day she was sure she'd never be seen again.

It was what the dark voice inside her wanted. The dangerous whisper that told her death was the inevitable—and even desired—end.

Until Evie shifted and broke the voice's stranglehold. She snuggled closer, planting a little kiss against Ross's arm. "I know what you've got. You've got a mermaid soul hidden underneath your know-it-all brain."

Ross stretched her hand out towards the reflection of the sun and watched its patterns dance across her skin. It *did* look like she was made of the twinkling magic from Triton's trident, though really, she knew it was only keratinocytes, and beneath that, an abundance of tissue, follicles, and fat.

Reality was unromantic.

Ross sighed. "I doubt that. Even if you want to believe you and Mom are mermaids, I'm not." She couldn't keep the weariness out of her voice. Nor could she keep the tears from her eyes. "I know I disappointed Mom. That she wanted me to be more like her, more like you. I could see it in the way she looked at me. The way *you* look at me." Ross dropped her arm to look at her sister. To *really* look at her, in a way that Ross hadn't been able to since their mom had died a year ago. "You have her eyes. Her hair. Her spirit. *Everything.*"

And Ross had nothing.

She had their father's Irish coloring, his blue eyes and red hair—not to mention his full-body freckles and long, wide nose. Evie, on the other hand, had inherited all their mother's soft features, like her round nose and gentle smile. And Evie's dark eyes, long lashes, and curly hair were to die for.

Ross tried to wipe her tears with her already-damp arm, but it did little good. "I was nothing but a disappointment."

"No! No, Ross. That's not true." Evie hugged Ross so firmly that Ross found it hard to breathe. "You didn't disappoint Mom."

"Yes, I did. I think . . . I think she was afraid of me. Of my temper. Like some sort of domesticated but dangerous shark that might eat you without warning." All of Ross's fears rushed back in full force. "The angry, combative child who made her life miserable."

"She didn't think you were a shark!" Evie's grip tightened and she buried her head into Ross's side. "She *loved* you."

"Not as much as she loved you." The tsunami of unresolved feelings surrounding Mom's life and death reared its head again, so tangible that it almost blocked out all the light. It towered above the two girls, invisible to the naked eye but palpably present. "She never tried to connect with me like she did with you." There was no other way to finish the thought except to remind Evie that Ross and their mother had been like plutonium and uranium shaken up in an atomic bomb.

"Nuh-uh! Mom was *perfect*," Evie protested.

"Nobody's perfect. It only seems that way to you because you were her baby." Ross wiped at her eyes again. "You still believed all her fairy tales. Mom lived in this imaginary world inside her head. You're lucky you hadn't grown up yet. Then she would've found out she didn't have a use for you anymore either." Ross had found *that* out when she suddenly became a gangly teenager, all awkward and hormonal. With a little kid around, especially one as cute as Evie, Ross hadn't been able to compete.

"Or maybe *you* didn't have a use for her." Evie straightened her legs out in front of her and flexed her toes. "Because Mom was a mermaid, and you can't just study mermaids and wonder how their gills work or what their bone structure looks like. You have to . . ." A few seconds passed as Evie seemed to flounder for the right words. "Be with them. Love them. Even if you don't understand them."

The silence stretched between them for a while. The noises of nature chattered all the louder because of it: the *swish, swoosh* of the lapping water, the crunching and shifting of the trees and their inhabitants.

"She *loved* you, Ross. No matter how many times you guys fought. She loved you."

"How?" Ross's voice faltered. She knew from her endless internet searches that she shouldn't foist her grief off on a younger child, shouldn't force Evie to play some parentified role. But right now, Ross needed to voice the childlike fears, and Evie seemed to be the vessel that held all their mother's knowledge. "I grew up. I didn't believe in magic, never listened to her stories, yelled at her all the time for being flighty and ridiculous . . ."

Evie took Ross's hand in her own. "That stuff didn't matter. She *did* love you. She told me so. She always said how proud she was of you. How smart you were, even if sometimes she thought you were *too* smart." Evie's mouth quirked into a wry smile. "She said that a lot."

Ross snorted.

"And she believed in you." Evie tilted her head. "She always knew you were special, just like a mermaid, even if you didn't believe in them."

Ross looked down as Evie intertwined their fingers. "And that's okay. It's okay if you don't believe that Mom is a mermaid, or if you don't believe she loves you. Because I do. I know she's coming back. But most of all, *I know* how much she loves you. And I know how much *I* love you." Evie leaned her head against Ross's arm, and Ross leaned over to press her cheek against the top of Evie's hair. The world around them smelled like fish and sunshine and water and trees—an earthy essence that would be embedded in Ross's memory forever.

She squeezed Evie's hand three times, a gesture that Evie returned.

Evie burrowed in closer. "That's mermaid for *'I love you,'* too, you know? That's how Mom knew it and why she taught it to us. She had to go for some urgent mermaid business, but she'll be back. We just have to keep hunting for mermaids until she does."

Suddenly, Evie gasped and sat up straighter, the top of her head bumping against Ross's. "I saw it! I saw a tail! My mermaid, Ross. She's back!" Evie slid off the rocky inlet and into the water. "Let's go—we have to go before she disappears!"

Ross stared out across the lake as her sister swam through the flickering sunlit waves. Maybe she should remind her sister this was nothing besides a fanciful daydream. But today, right now, Ross didn't have the heart. For the first time in a long time, her sister's smile broke through the numbness and allowed some hope to shine on her weary soul. Maybe mermaids were real—and maybe they weren't. But one thing was certain: a bit of their mom would be with them forever, if only in Evie's spirit.

Ross slid into the water. "All right. Let's go catch a mermaid."

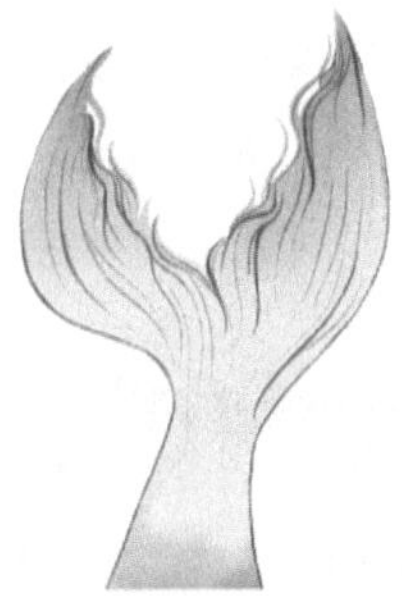

FINS FOR FREEDOM

Humans are vile, selfish enslavers whose crimes must be stopped"—that was the motto of *Fins for Freedom*, Caribe's tiny band of mermaid freedom fighters. And by *tiny* . . . she was technically the only member. But what the group lacked in numbers and a catchy slogan, she made up for in spirit.

A bright orange fish darted away from Caribe as her fin sliced through the water, her mind on her mission.

She'd heard horror stories about humans from all her friends in school. One boy's father had lost an arm to a boat motor; one girl thought her second cousin twice-removed had been snagged by one of the humans' mermaid-catching hooks and lost an eye.

But the worst of the worst stories all revolved around Busselton Jetty in Western Australia. Caribe had seen it once as a small child, only seven years old, when curiosity had gotten the best of her and some friends. They'd swum as near as they could to the humans' territory. The long, wooden jetty marked the boundary between the human and mermaid worlds. The jetty jutted straight out into the ocean for miles, held up by thick posts that descended into the ocean. Barnacles, seaweed, and algae decorated the wood, and lights on various posts illuminated the dark blue water.

And that's when Caribe had seen them first. *Captured mermaids.*

"I hear the humans force the mermaids to perform for them every summer," Waverly had whispered as the girls peeked out of a coral cave to catch a glimpse of Busselton Jetty. "My sister says she knows someone who got caught. I think it was her friend's aunt's cousin's daughter?"

Caribe shivered, the water suddenly chilly against her skin. "Did they ever find her again?"

"Never," Waverly said, eyes wide. "The mermaids all disappear from Busselton Jetty at the end of summer. And they're never … seen … *again.*" Waverly wiggled her fingers, which every seven-year-old knew added extra spookiness to a story.

Caribe's bottom lip trembled. She didn't like the thought of disappearing. She'd miss her parents, her home, and her pod too much, and the thought of other people missing *their* families weighed on her heart. "But why don't they just swim away? It's the wide open ocean. They don't have to stay there!"

Waverly bobbed her head. "Yes, they do." She peered over the coral and pointed. "See the ones over there? The ones dressed in the orca skins?"

Caribe raised her eyes just enough to see what Waverly meant. Sure enough, Caribe spied a few humans in the water, all of them dressed in black suits that reminded her of massive orcas. "Uh-huh."

"Those are the prison guards. They're so strong they killed the whales just to wear their skin. Every summer, they're the ones that capture new mermaids and hold them there." Waverly turned to face Caribe with a somber, all-knowing expression. "That's what Jetsam from the north pod told me."

Terror slithered down Caribe's spine and made her shudder. If Jetsam *and* Waverly said it was so, then it *had* to be true. And someone needed to go help those mermaids, to set them free so they could return to their families before they disappeared like Waverly's sister's friend's aunt's cousin's daughter.

Caribe had created Fins for Freedom right then. One day, she'd resolved, she would return and free all those poor mermaids, when she had grown up a bit more and could fight off the orca-skin guards. And, after six years of planning, *today* was that day. It didn't matter that her parents had told her to stay away countless times and insisted that she'd be safe if she just kept her distance from the humans and Busselton Jetty. Because it wasn't about her safety—it was about doing what needed to be done to save others.

Even if the thought of the jetty *still* filled Caribe with some trepidation. She gulped as she caught her first peek of those thick slabs of wood—prison bars, although they didn't physically capture all the mermaids. Deep breaths. She had to focus on deep breaths as she swam from coral to coral until she could make out every detail of the jetty, down to the colorful barnacles attached to the wood.

Sunlight streamed down and illuminated the beautiful—but macabre—scene. The brilliant iridescent fins of her kinfolk gleamed as the mermaids swam between the posts . . . and the *humans.*

All shapes and sizes of humans. Some of them wore nothing but flimsy leg clothes. Others—mostly the females—had shells, too. A handful of humans hid inside something Jetsam from the northern pod called an "underwater observatory," a huge, circular building filled with glass where humans could gawk at their mermaid prisoners.

And, of course, surrounding all the mermaids were the guards, still clad in their orca skins. Because of them, Caribe had never been able to get close enough to talk to the captured mermaids. But today, she'd rush in and tell them that they didn't have to stay in prison. If they all swam at once, they could get out and return to their pods and the families who loved them.

Caribe wouldn't let another mermaid disappear like Waverly's sister's friend's aunt's cousin's daughter.

"All right, Caribe." She curled her fingers around one of the tall pieces of coral. "You can do this." She'd begged her parents to enroll her in all kinds of after-school self-defense classes in preparation for today. She'd waited and tracked the human crowds and the mermaids' schedules. Now—two weeks into these new mermaids' captivity—would be the best time to free them.

She allowed herself a few more deep breaths to steady herself—

One of the orca-attackers brought something to his eye. A sleek, black machine with a long, round nose.

A gun.

That looked *exactly* like how Jetsam had described the guns to Waverly and Caribe: handheld, black, and with a part that stuck out in front. These horrific monsters would use guns to slaughter Caribe's kinfolk, just as they had murdered the poor whales to wear their skins.

Caribe didn't think. Her terror forced her into action, and she bellowed, "Stop!" Shoving off the coral, she barreled between the innocent mermaid and her attacker and batted the gun away with her fluke. The human lost his grip on the weapon and bent down to catch it. Caribe's heart pulsated like a trapped guppy. If she let him retrieve his weapon, he'd turn it on her. With a wrench of her abdomen, Caribe swung her tail up and smacked the human's face with it.

Chaos erupted all around them.

Both humans and enslaved merfolk screamed. Some of the mermaids swam toward her, probably thankful for their newfound freedom. Others bolted toward the observatory—those poor, unfortunate souls who apparently believed captivity was their only choice in life. The attempted murderer put his hand against his head. All around Caribe, more orca warriors raised their guns, and lights flashed from the tops of the weapons.

She had to get the captive mermaids out, *now*. The humans were about to slaughter them all.

Another human grabbed Caribe's upper arms, but she hadn't been top of her self-defense class for nothing. She drove one elbow up into his chin; he made a strange, muffled noise and released her. Using her torque, she slammed her tail into his side. The sharp scales caught against his orca skin and tore it.

A thrill shot through Caribe. Vindication for the orcas *and* mermaids.

More humans—some in the flimsy shells and leg cloths, some in the orca skins—flocked to the water. They came from the jetty, from the surface, *everywhere*.

"Swim!" Caribe yelled. "Mermaids, if we all swim into the deeper waters together, they can't stop us!" She ducked out of the way of humans and repeated her message several times, but no mermaid heeded her message. They all turned toward the surface or jetty, save one lonely soul close to Caribe. The straggler's blue eyes were wide, mouth agape.

Innocent. Scared. Just like Waverly's sister's friend's aunt's cousin's daughter would have been.

There was no time to get all the other mermaids; Caribe would have to come back for them. But if she didn't leave now, she'd be joining them here in this prison.

There'd only be one rescue today.

With a growl, Caribe latched onto the shocked girl's hand and dragged her into the wild blue. Caribe's heart pounded in her ears; her face grew flushed. Hopefully, in all the pandemonium, the two of them would be able to slip away unnoticed, lest they end up captured like Waverly's sister's friend's aunt's cousin's daughter.

Caribe darted from coral to coral, dragging the other mermaid along. She'd learned in school that coral was good camouflage for mermaid tails, and she'd set the place where she and Waverly had hidden as children as her rendezvous point. The two of them could finally talk there, and Caribe could explain everything to the traumatized girl.

The large pink-and-orange piece of coral that stretched wider than three mermaids in either direction beckoned Caribe. She jerked her freed mermaid behind its beautiful prongs. They could stay here for a while, until the commotion died down. But the new girl had other ideas. She wrenched away from Caribe and pumped her arms furiously toward the surface.

"No! Are you crazy? They could see you if you go up there!" Caribe shrieked.

The other mermaid didn't reply.

"Barnacles," Caribe muttered. She peeked up over the coral to gauge the distance from the chaos. Busselton Jetty was a few hundred meters away . . . If she was quick, she could probably grab the girl and yank her back to safety without anyone noticing.

The confused mermaid had already surfaced by the time Caribe took after her. With one swift tug to the arm, Caribe wrenched the girl back under the waves—only for the girl to elbow Caribe in the head and heave *her*, stunned, into the open air.

"Don't! We have to get *down* before anyone sees us!" Caribe snapped, right as the girl bellowed, "What do you think you're doing, kid?"

The mermaid spoke with the strong vowel accent of the land-dwellers. She must have been exposed to them for a long time to have adopted their accent, which was far different from the mermaids'.

"What is *wrong* with you?" the girl demanded. "I didn't even think we hired kids as young as you—is this some kind of *joke* to you? Do you want to get fired? You assaulted a customer back there!"

"I don't care about getting *fired*!" Whatever that meant. "I care about your *freedom*. These people kidnapped you!"

"What?" The girl's dark eyebrows rose. "Nobody's kidnapped anyone. I've worked here for three years—paid my way through uni." She scowled. "Are . . . are *you* kidnapped? Is something not on the up and up?" She shoved some damp hair strands away from her dazzling blue eyes; their color was as bright as the ocean waves. A sure sign of mer heritage, of a deep connection to the sea.

The same color as Caribe's.

"No, *I'm* not kidnapped. *You* and all those other mermaids were kidnapped by humans! They make you perform here at this prison for one summer before they kill you! I should know. My friend Waverly's friend's aunt's cousin's daughter got taken by humans." Caribe tucked one of her auburn curls behind her ear. The despicable human air was already making it frizz up. "That's why Fins for Freedom exists."

The girl narrowed her eyes. "Do you think I'm a flamin' galah? Is this for some telly prank show?"

The two girls stared at each other, fins flicking, churning their arms to keep themselves afloat. Unfamiliar words danced in Caribe's mind before sinking to the bottom of her stomach like rocks. "I . . . I don't understand what you mean." She glanced over the girl's shoulder, but no humans had appeared on the horizon yet. "The humans. They had you surrounded by jailers in orca skins. They kidnapped you from your pod, and—"

"I'm a *worker*. They *pay* me to entertain the guests, and those aren't jailers. They're just scuba divers. You don't really think I'm a mermaid, do you?" The girl barked out a laugh, only for it to die when Caribe didn't join in. "You . . . think I'm a real mermaid?" The girl tugged at the waist of her tail, which pulled away from her skin with ease. "It's silicone. See?"

The rocks in the pit of Caribe's stomach grew heavier. "You . . . you aren't? You're human?"

"Of course. Just like you." The girl reached out, and her fingers brushed against Caribe's waistline. But her fingers found no grip there, as the scales and ivory-colored skin blended seamlessly. The human-with-a-tail paled until all her freckles stood out. "You . . . that . . . your tail . . . you're a *real* mermaid?"

"I . . ." Caribe's mouth dried. Her mind reeled with a hundred horror stories about humans. This was some kind of trick. A kind of cruel game where humans disguised themselves as mermaids only to kidnap them, like sharks impersonating dolphins. Had Jetsam or Waverly known this? Was that how the humans got Waverly's sister's aunt's friend's cousin's daughter?

Caribe's breath hitched. The air—it felt too heavy. Too much. But she couldn't stop, couldn't stop breathing it. She wanted to get back to her home—her family—her friends—she didn't want to spend the rest of her life in some sort of circus.

She whirled around, poised to dive beneath the waves.

"Wait—" The human lunged across the water, and Caribe shrieked.

"Don't hurt me!" Caribe splashed the girl, but then wished she'd used her tail to attack instead. As if a handful of water droplets could be a protection barrier. So much for all her self-defense classes. She was about as quick as an unhatched egg in a real crisis.

The girl sputtered and shook her head. "Easy, kid! Just—just calm down. You're the flamin' *mermaid* here! Why . . . How could *I* hurt you?"

"Easy! You're—you're human. You murder mers and . . . and keep us in fish tanks and . . . the *jetty*—"

"Busselton Jetty is a tourist attraction. Nobody's ever murdered anyone there . . . at least, not yet. But if Jake the clerk tries to flirt with me again, you never know." The human's voice softened, and she let out a high-pitched laugh, one that sounded like it might actually be a hysterical cry. Caribe could understand. She felt the same way right now.

If Caribe had any good sense, she'd swim away and give up Fins for Freedom forever. Yet for some reason, she babbled on like a prawn. "But the man in the orca skin—he had a *gun*. He tried to shoot you! I saw the lights and everything when he took aim!"

"I told you, he's a scuba diver. And he had a waterproof camera." The human rubbed her temple. "He wasn't trying to hurt me. He . . . uh, was trying to tell me I was doing a great job. Take a picture."

New words floated around Caribe's head until she wanted to vomit up the metaphorical rocks in her stomach. Waverly had never told Caribe anything about this. *Nobody* in school had. "But . . ." her voice trailed off. She could only stare, gaping like a codfish, as her entire worldview shattered. Maybe one of them should have had the common sense to swim away from this strange encounter. Or maybe they each had a million thoughts but couldn't act on a single one of them, too thunderstruck to do anything intelligent.

Finally, the girl spoke. "Name's Em." Her voice cracked a bit. "What's yours? And where's your mum?"

"Caribe. And my mum's back at home," Caribe mumbled. "She thinks I'm out with my friend Waverly, but Waverly's home sick."

Em let out another long breath and closed her eyes, muttering to herself. "I can't believe this. I'm talking to a mermaid kid, or a kid that thinks they're a mermaid and has the most convincing tail I've ever seen." She rubbed her temple. "Listen. I'm not going to hurt you. Nobody in Busselton is going to hurt you. Nobody's kidnapping anybody."

"But the *stories*." Caribe gulped. "It's not just Busselton Jetty. There's—there's even mermaid hooks to catch young guppies who wander away from their mothers. And if you're not careful, a fisherman might take you over to a place called an *ack-quarry-um* so humans can stare at you all day. Or a museum, where they'll kill you and put your body on display. That's why I founded Fins for Freedom. To stop that."

The girl's face twisted into a frown. "Well, humans have stories too. Like mermaid sirens luring sailors to their deaths. Or killing people with their sharp, vicious teeth."

"We don't do any of that!" Caribe touched her lips, which covered her decidedly normal teeth that didn't look too different from Em's—though Caribe *had* lost a tooth recently, so maybe a gap in her smile would look odd to a human.

"Listen, the point was that—I'm starting to think maybe the stories aren't right. Or, at least, to some extent, because the stories *do* say mermaids exist." Em let out a long laugh again. "I don't know. Maybe all the oxygen got cut off to my brain and I'm dying on the ocean floor." She raked her fingers through her hair. "Point is, you say you're a mermaid scared about humans hurting you, and I'm here to tell you that I'm not gonna hurt you. I just wanna get you back to your mum."

Waves rolled between them as the tide brought them closer together.

Cool sea air blew against Caribe's bare shoulders, and she shivered. She would have wrapped some kelp around herself if she'd known she'd be on the surface. "So . . . so nobody was kidnapped and held prisoner at Busselton Jetty or *ack-quarry-ums*?" Then what had really happened to Waverly's friend's aunt's cousin's daughter? Did she even *exist*?

Em leaned backward and raised her phony fluke. Up close, Caribe noticed how distorted it looked—stiffer and oddly shaped, probably to make a place for the feet. "Nope. The only mermaids in Busselton I know of are fake, like me. We get paid." She lowered her fake tail back into the water. Then she licked her lips, though she made a sour face when she did. "Listen . . . if you ever want someone to tell you about what the human world is actually like, I could help you. That way you don't do anything dangerous again, like go barging into Busselton Jetty. We could be mates."

Caribe wrinkled her nose. That was a new term, too. "What?"

"I mean a—a friend. Or whatever mermaids call the people they like to hang out with. Swim with, talk about stuff."

"Oh." For the first time that day, Caribe felt a hint of a smile tugging on her lips. "We call them friends, too."

"See? That's one thing mermaids and humans have in common." Em stuck her hand out. "Do you shake hands underwater to agree to something?"

"Yes, sometimes." Caribe clasped Em's fingers.

"Another thing we share, then." Em grinned, so big and bright it lit up her ocean-blue eyes.

The two shook on it.

As their hands dropped back to their sides, Em glanced back towards land. "All right. I'll go back to the jetty and tell them . . . something. Don't worry, though. I'll tell them you were just some local ankle-biter playing a prank so they don't come looking for proof of a real mermaid."

A blush overtook Caribe's cheeks until it felt like the sun itself glowed from inside her. "Thanks, but I didn't bite your ankle."

"No—it means a kid. You."

"Oh." What a weird term, especially considering Caribe hadn't *ever* bitten an ankle. She didn't even know what an ankle *was*. But whatever it was, it was weird human kids did it so much. "What do I do, then? Just go home?" She furrowed her brow. "I've been obsessed with Busselton Jetty for years. But if none of the mermaids at Busselton are in danger, what do I do? That means Fins for Freedom doesn't have a purpose."

"Well, sure it does. There are still lots of things to fight for. There's a lot wrong with this world, on land and in the sea." Em swept her arms back and forth. "Who knows. Maybe I can help you figure out something. Be your land ambassador. If your mum says it's okay, we can meet for brekky tomorrow morning and chat. Somewhere safe, away from humans."

"Well, maybe, but—what's brekky?"

"Breakfast."

Caribe's eyes widened. Breakfast with a human? The kids at school would never believe her. "Can I bring Waverly, too, if she's feeling better? She'll be *so* shocked I met a real human."

"As long as *both* your mums say it's okay or come with you." Em held up her pinky. "I'm going to teach you a solemn human oath, all right? You can't break it. It's called a pinky swear. Watch." Carefully, she guided both their fingers together until they linked and curled around each other. "No more going back to the human world by yourself. Big sister Em's orders. Promise."

Caribe gave Em's pinky a shake. "I promise." Unlike Waverly, she'd never had a big sister before, but the thought of having a *human* one seemed pretty cool, and she had to grin.

"Perf," Em said. "Meet me at the jetty and we'll find a safe strip of beach for us to talk. I'll bring some bikkies, and this time, we *won't* assault people."

Caribe frowned. "Bikkies?"

"Biscuits," Em clarified. "We usually don't have them for breakfast, but I'll make an exception for you. Because if you don't have them underwater, they'll blow your mind." A pause. "That's a human expression. They won't actually hurt you."

"Oh, good."

Em leaned over and ruffled Caribe's hair, which only made it frizzier. A small price to pay, though, to have a friend—a *mate*, as Em had said—in the human world. "I'll see you tomorrow, Caribe. Stay out of trouble."

"I'll try." Caribe waved as her new friend drifted away. "See you tomorrow for, um . . . brekky and bikkies."

"You're sounding like a real Aussie now." Em waved back before she turned to swim back toward the jetty.

Smiling, Caribe dove under the water and set off for home, her heart lighter with the promise of bikkies, brekkies, and new mates.

Maybe humans weren't quite so vile and selfish after all.

She'd have to change her motto.

SHARP
AS A
SIREN'S SONG

Whether on land or sea, Lady Ambrosia knew there to be one indisputable fact: women always finished the wars men started.

Lady Ambrosia's inky octopus tentacles slithered across the lithe white-haired mermaid's form. The Sea Witch lifted the dying mermaid's chin as the younger girl seized on the ocean floor. "You failed me," the Sea Witch hissed. "You were my legs and ears on the surface, and you failed. You had *one month* to kill the king of Iylamor. One month to sabotage their defenses and exploit their weaknesses. That was more than generous. Indeed, the most generous I have *ever* been."

The white-haired mermaid coughed. Green blood drifted from her mouth, and the tides swept it out of Lady Ambrosia's underwater grotto and into the open ocean. "King Cyrillus . . . didn't do anything . . . anything wrong." The mermaid spat another globule of emerald blood, her teeth stained with the liquid as she bared them at the Sea Witch. "*Isn't* right."

In the dark corners of the room—the shadows where the light of the glow stones couldn't reach—one of the other mermaids whimpered. Lady Ambrosia smirked. Good—she hoped her other girls watched. She hoped this image seared itself into their minds and replayed in their sleep so they never even *dreamed* of disobeying her.

"I didn't ask you to philosophize." Lady Ambrosia wrapped a tentacle around the mermaid's throat and tightened, raising the girl higher off the ground. The chit gasped and clawed at the supple surface, as pathetically weak and ineffective as a child. "I told you to assassinate that man and sabotage his kingdom or my poison would kill you."

The mermaid's eyes flickered to the antidote, which rested on a shelf carved into the cavern wall. The red liquid frothed and bubbled inside the corked bottle like a turbulent crimson sea.

The mermaid's tail flailed as she tried to loosen the tentacle slowly choking her. She managed to pry it away from her windpipe just enough to wheeze, "Won't . . . won't kill an innocent man."

"You act as if you have a choice." Lady Ambrosia's tentacle constricted, drawing the girl closer. "I've been paid by Briglen's monarch to end the dispute over the sea border, and I always keep my word. I already sent another girl to assassinate him; she's surfacing right now. The king of Iylamor will die, regardless of who holds the knife." Lady Ambrosia plucked a dagger of cerulean sea glass from the stalagmite table to her right.

The mermaid writhed. Her fluke knocked over an empty cauldron and the coral podium next to it. A book of spells tumbled from the podium onto the floor, its seaweed pages fluttering in the currents.

"Remember this. All of you." Lady Ambrosia's gaze roved to each of the other girls. She would not be made a fool of again. She was their *god*; their very lives were owed to her. "You are all here because of your debts, because your family needed my magic. But remember this." Lady Ambrosia hoisted the wriggling traitor higher. "You cannot escape me until you have repaid everything in full. And if you disobey, your lives are forfeit."

The crowd of girls shrank behind the natural cavern columns or into shadowed recesses. Not a single one tried to help their friend.

A smile flickered across Ambrosia's face. Excellent.

She turned her attention back to the white-haired mermaid. "Was your life really worth saving that doomed king's? Or . . . oh, I know. Perhaps it was that little prince. Maybe I should have my new girl kill him as well. I think Briglen had plans for him, but I doubt they would be very upset if all of Iylamor's ruling family fell beneath my knife."

The girl's blue eyes burned as if they possessed a fire that would incinerate the Sea Witch. Her fingers dug into Lady Ambrosia's tentacles, though the Sea Witch didn't feel the pathetic attack.

". . . Hope you *choke* on . . . your machinations," the girl rasped. Flecks of blood emphasized every slow syllable.

Lady Ambrosia pressed the dagger against the mermaid's breast. "And *I* hope your sister isn't quite as mouthy as you. She'll be your replacement in my ranks. I don't think the orphanage will make a fuss if I claim one tiny ten-year-old."

"Don't . . . touch . . . Wisteria!"

Ah. So she had found the soft underbelly of this white-haired girl after all. Perhaps a cold rush of fear might extinguish this mermaid's inner flame. "Your parents' debts survive even though they don't, and you couldn't pay. Why shouldn't I go after your sister?"

"No!" the girl choked out, her voice low and rough. She tried to claw at Lady Ambrosia's face but couldn't reach. "*Monster!*"

A few whimpers came from the girls hiding in the corners. All of them had loved ones. All would know how futile it was to escape the fury of a self-made god.

"No." Lady Ambrosia leaned in until her lips touched the mermaid's ear. "I'm a Sea Witch, love."

With that, Lady Ambrosia shoved the dagger into the mermaid's heart. The girl's eyes widened, the sea turning emerald around them as blood coiled into the tide. The fire in the girl's eyes dulled to a smolder, a single ember holding onto a spark of resentment even as life drained from her body.

The Sea Witch yanked her knife out of the girl's chest and set the body free to drift in the water. From the darkened corners of the grotto, silent mermaids poked their heads out.

"Remember this moment, girls." Lady Ambrosia turned to stare at each face in turn. "No one betrays me and lives."

"Yes, Lady Ambrosia," a few of them murmured. Others bobbed their heads in agreement; a handful merely watched in horror as the tides carried their friend's body out of the grotto.

"Good. Do your jobs for me until your contracts are paid in full, and you and your families will be safe." Her threat made, Lady Ambrosia propelled herself out of the grotto, sealing the exit with a spell. As she faced the open ocean, a lean smile curved her lips.

Now, to fetch a certain little mermaid.

～～～

Lady Ambrosia had gone up to Witch Rock today.

Wisteria held her breath and squeezed her eyes shut for exactly thirty seconds. Her heart echoed in her ears, but she persevered. Logically, Wisteria *knew* her little rituals didn't affect the outcome of anything. But they gave her a modicum of control over her tumultuous existence, which in turn strengthened her determination to survive every horrible day she'd faced in the past decade.

Witch Rock days meant Lady Ambrosia had a customer. Customers meant assassinations. Hence, the ritual. If Wisteria didn't want to be picked for an assassination today, she had to hold her breath and close her eyes for exactly thirty seconds. After that, she'd be able to inhale more oxygen-rich water. Her rituals had worked every time before, but she could never relax her guard. Never be *too* careful.

Twenty-eight, twenty-nine . . . thirty.

Just in time.

The Sea Witch swam back into the grotto, propelled by her long black tentacles. "Well, girls. This is certainly an interesting turn of events."

Wisteria traced the edge of a scale on her gold-and-black tail.

"Some of you may remember that about ten years ago, Briglen paid me to assassinate the king of Iylamor. The job was carried out, though one of my girls betrayed me and was killed for it." Lady Ambrosia stopped by the cauldron and flicked through the pages of her spellbook.

Oh, no.

Wisteria gulped. The Iylamor debacle had been *Primrose's* final mission. The reason why Wisteria had been stuck here for the last miserable decade, why she'd lost her childhood and teenage years to a monster.

Now more than ever, Wisteria couldn't blink and break eye contact—that would only risk inciting Lady Ambrosia's wrath. But Wisteria's mind said if she couldn't close her eyes, she could hold her breath for forty seconds and it would reinforce the magic. Wisteria wouldn't be chosen.

She wouldn't be punished for her elder sister's failure.

But just to be sure, maybe Wisteria needed to hold her breath until her lungs cried out.

"Unfortunately, Iylamor did not fall, though its king did. My client believed the death of Iylamor's beloved king would crush the nation's rebellion and give Briglen access to the seaboard. However, Iylamor has proved scrappier than anticipated, and the war has raged on these last ten years." Lady Ambrosia emptied a purple vial into her cauldron and a puff of smoke wafted upward. "Remember, girls. Women—*my* women, my *assassins*—always end wars men start." Her black eyes locked with Wisteria's golden ones. "This is the only war I have failed to end."

Wisteria's shoulders ached where they'd been tense for so long. Lady Ambrosia could not fight against her inner rituals. Everything would be all right. Except . . .

"Iylamor's prince has now come of age and will be crowned king on his twenty-first birthday. He is the only son of the former king, and, as such, there is enormous pressure to produce an heir. This has pushed him to make a hasty decision. He is throwing a ball where he will meet all eligible ladies and choose one to be his bride." Lady Ambrosia dropped a white-plumed anemone into her cauldron; another puff of smoke burst out like it had been propelled from an underwater vent.

Lungs. Burning. Must. Breathe.

Wisteria gave in and gasped—praying the small breath wouldn't break her ritual's magic.

"If we kill him before he finds a wife, we can eliminate the rest of the royal bloodline. Our client will be able to end this war, Iylamor will come under Briglen's command, and my good reputation as a purveyor of the finest assassins will be redeemed." Lady Ambrosia's eyes swept the room. "One of you will infiltrate the ball and attempt to win the prince's heart. When his guard is down, you are to kill him."

The girls remained quiet. Wisteria held her breath again. From her head down to her tailbones, she *knew*: everything hinged on this moment. If she broke the silence, she would be chosen.

Heartbeats passed. She prayed that small breath she'd taken moments before wouldn't doom her. If she gave in to her protesting lungs now, it'd be a disaster. Her rituals had never failed her before. If she held out, they would keep her safe once more.

But as time stretched, her lungs started to scream. *Breathe!*

One quick inhale wouldn't hurt.

She gulped down one frantic breath of air.

"Wisteria," Lady Ambrosia said with a vindictive smile. Wisteria jerked her head up, staring as the witch continued, "This mission is personal for you. After all, your sister refused to kill this prince's father. Because of *her* failure, you had to take on your family's debt."

"Primrose didn't—" Wisteria cut herself off and cursed the familial love that might have just sealed her fate. Her white hair drifted in front of her face and obscured her view of the Sea Witch.

"You think she didn't do anything wrong? She's the reason you're in this mess, little mermaid." Lady Ambrosia leaned forward. "She'd almost repaid your parents' debt, you know. She almost earned her freedom. But she chose to save some poor stranger and sacrifice *you* instead."

Wisteria's cheeks flushed. "But . . ."

Lady Ambrosia grabbed a clam from a shelf, cracked it, and tossed it into her cauldron. As her hand circled over the concoction, she began a low incantation. The atmosphere in the room thickened—though it was hard to tell if that was because of Wisteria's perception or the witch's magic. But every breath she heaved felt like an orca whale settling on her lungs.

"I'll tell you what." The Sea Witch's hand paused mid-flourish. "If you murder the crown prince, we'll consider your family's debt paid. You'll be free."

Free.

The word spun in Wisteria's mind until she felt dizzy. *Free.* She mouthed it, and its silent promise tasted sweet on her tongue. She hadn't been free in ten years. Lady Ambrosia controlled when her girls woke, ate, slept. When they could leave the grotto—which only happened when the Sea Witch needed an unlucky mermaid to kill someone. It had been a decade since Wisteria had seen the sun . . .

"But . . . you've never trained me with the other girls." Wisteria's tongue felt heavy and her heart hammered.

Lady Ambrosia tapped her chin. "Oh? Have I not?" A smile tugged her lips upward. "I guess I became too busy after your sister betrayed me. What a shame *she* couldn't teach you. The feisty little chit was one of my best assassins." She stretched a tentacle toward Wisteria, and it circled her wrist. With a single jerk, Lady Ambrosia dragged Wisteria to float beside her, next to the cauldron.

"This poison will give you legs from sunrise to midnight each day. But there's one small change to this arrangement. I gave your sister a month, and she used that month to betray me. You will get no such mercy. This batch of poison will kill you in three days. Assassinate the prince, and I'll give you the antidote. If you fail me, you will die." Lady Ambrosia's claw-like fingers seized Wisteria's face, holding firm when Wisteria tried to wrench away. "Do you understand?"

The Sea Witch wasn't offering Wisteria a choice on whether to take the mission, but if she had, would Wisteria have turned down this opportunity? Could she easily discard this one shot at freedom solely because she had to kill someone?

Of course, if she had a *real* choice, she'd pick freedom without anyone's death. But that would never be an option offered to her, unless she had a fairy godmother like one of the girls in her childhood stories. But she wasn't important enough to garner the attention of the fairies—just the ire of the Sea Witch. And, now that Wisteria thought about it, what if she was never picked for another mission again and had to spend the rest of her days languishing underground, a slave to Lady Ambrosia?

The Sea Witch scooped a ladle of the poisonous potion and pushed the edge between Wisteria's lips. The brew tasted sour, burning as Wisteria choked it down. The searing sensation only seemed to intensify on its journey; it felt like hot liquid iron inside her. But the pain didn't stop at her stomach—it twisted all the way down to the tip of her tail.

Wisteria doubled over and clutched her middle. Lady Ambrosia's tentacle tightened around her wrist as the Sea Witch rocketed out of the grotto, dragging Wisteria behind her.

Up, up, up they went. If only Wisteria could appreciate the multicolored fish, the towering coral, and the way the water lightened as they drew closer to the surface. But she could only cry out as the fire inside her worsened. She'd seen enough of the other girls' transformations to know she wouldn't die, but apparently she could creep up to the brink of death and still live.

Her lungs twisted and tightened. The oxygen underwater seemed to feel thicker, as though she was drinking it instead of breathing it, and Wisteria held her breath and pretended this was merely another one of her rituals. That if she waged war against her desire for air and won, this would all be a nightmare and she'd wake up back in the Sea Witch's cave.

The surface inched closer.

Finally, they broke through the waves, and Lady Ambrosia tossed Wisteria onto Witch Rock. Wisteria rolled, yelping as pebbles scraped her body. She crashed into a jutting peak and lay there, disoriented, wishing she could claw the flame out of her body.

Her scales dried up even faster in the sun, and soon the only sign she'd even been a mermaid at all were the tiny gold-and-black flecks across her legs. She'd have to hide those when she entered the palace.

But— *Triton*, those legs. Wisteria poked them each in turn. She tried to associate each new part with something she was familiar with. The toes, for example, replaced the fluke of her tail; maybe she could wiggle them. The knobby knees were awkward. And even though she was used to bending her tail, bending these legs just felt *wrong*.

"Yes, yes. They're a fine pair of legs," Lady Ambrosia snapped. She bobbed along in the waves, just out of reach, only the lower half of her body submerged. "A fine pair of man-catching legs."

"Men find them attractive?" Wisteria wrinkled her nose. "But . . . why?"

"You will find there are a lot of strange things people find attractive." Lady Ambrosia cackled, but Wisteria couldn't understand what had been so humorous. Her face flushed. She would never survive among these humans.

Before her brain could tell her to stop, Wisteria pleaded, "Please, can't *you* go, Lady Ambrosia? You know more about the land-dwellers than me. And you actually *want* this boy dead." Wisteria wrapped her arms around herself and shivered. "And you know how to kill people." Not to mention, Lady Ambrosia probably *enjoyed* that activity.

"Why would I poison myself?" The Sea Witch clucked her tongue and rolled her eyes. "Mermaids aren't supposed to have legs. Whenever you're on land, not only will you have pain from my magic in you, but every step will be torturous." She snickered. "Why do you think I need slaves like you in the first place?"

Lady Ambrosia turned away, but Wisteria let out a sharp cry. "Wait! Won't I need clothes?" Her voice trembled. She only wore her seaweed-and-seashell corset, which left her with scant protection.

"Well, darling, I dare say being naked as a bluefish might be one way to win the prince's heart, but you'd never get past the palace guards." Lady Ambrosia waved her hand. "Don't worry. I'll take care of that. After all, you can't go to the ball without a magnificent gown." The Sea Witch's dark eyes twinkled—an unnerving sight. "I bought it from one of the Briglen duchesses for you. Don't you feel so special? It's on the other side of the peak, waiting for you. I'll go get it right now." Smirking, she dipped lower into the waves. "Just consider me your fairy godmother."

~~~

For hours, the sun scorched Wisteria's skin and eyes as she baked on Witch Rock. Not only did the heat pain her, but her first attempts to walk ended in bloodied knees and pebbles embedded in her hands. But eventually, the moon glided into the sky while Wisteria stumbled across the sand toward the palace, Witch Rock far behind her. A white curl swung into her face, and she tucked it behind her ear. After returning with the dress, Lady Ambrosia had styled Wisteria's hair into an elegant updo, securing it with starfish, coral, and pearls. A gold-and-black ball gown—one that perfectly matched Wisteria's tail—trailed past her feet and covered the remnants of the scales on her legs.

Wisteria winced with every footfall, though—and not just because mermaids were not supposed to have legs and every step was like a knife jabbing into her soles. Lady Ambrosia had bequeathed Wisteria a pair of beautiful sea glass slippers, made for aesthetics—or perhaps some kind of cruel joke—and not for practicality.

A matching sea glass dagger pressed against her thigh.

Steeling herself, Wisteria kissed her fingers and pressed them against her ballgown—a traditional mermaid blessing for safety. She remembered
~~~

doing the same to her father and mother's cloaks before they would go out on errands when she was young. Back then, rituals had seemed like a game, not the anxious compulsion they'd become.

But they were all she had now.

To further distract herself from her terror, Wisteria took to counting each palace step once she reached the castle and started to ascend toward its large front doors. She had blessed herself. She would survive. Everything would be fine.

Twenty-eight, twenty-nine . . . twenty-nine?

Did the royals not have the decency to end their stairs on an even number?

Wisteria turned around and recounted. No, she'd tallied it correctly. Twenty-nine. An evil, odd number.

Her mission was doomed.

No, she mustn't think like that, despite the fact that the poison still churned inside of her and sent flashes of heat throughout her body. She whirled toward the doors once more, leaving her thoughts behind with those odd-numbered steps. Her mission would succeed, and she'd earn her freedom, and—

"*Ack!*" Wisteria crashed into something and reeled backward—right toward the stairs.

How ironic.

Those blasted, evil stairs would spell her doom after all.

"Careful!" The person she'd collided with grabbed her wrist and jerked her forward. Wisteria crashed into her savior's chest, her vision spinning.

"I'm so sorry," she breathed. "The—the steps. They had *twenty-nine . . .*"

The person chortled, a low, raspy sound, and Wisteria realized for the first time she'd stumbled straight into a young man. "Twenty-nine? Unacceptable. I shall have the servants start mixing concrete immediately."

Wisteria laughed, but the sound felt more nervous than sincere.

The young man steadied her before he tucked his hands behind his back. Wisteria cleared her throat and dropped her arms from around his neck, heat rising to her cheeks. He must not have shared her embarrassment, though, because he shifted his weight toward her, not away. He had a few inches on her, dark eyes, and a smooth face that didn't show any hint of a beard. She estimated him to be around her age, twenty, but he could have been older. "You look anxious. Don't worry; I am, too." He smirked. "I always feel like a fish out of water at these events."

Wisteria swallowed. What ritual did she have in her arsenal to protect her secret? She'd never expected a casual remark to toe so close to the shoreline. "I'm sure I don't know what you mean."

"Don't you?" The young man offered his arm, a formal invitation, by mermaid standards at least, to swim—*walk*?—with someone. "Hmm. Pardon me. You remind me very much of a dear friend of mine." His gaze roamed over her hair before he led her inside the marble palace doors. "When I spotted you from inside, I just had to come and meet you." He lowered his voice and leaned in closer, as if they were two friends sharing a secret. Wisteria's face flushed. "Maybe you know her? She's quite memorable, with hair as white as snow and eyes that blazed with blue fire."

The light of the golden chandelier blinded Wisteria.

Hair as white as snow.

A full orchestra overwhelmed her ears, and the *people*! After growing up in a grotto surrounded only by fifteen other girls, the crowd seemed suffocating.

Eyes that blazed with blue fire.

The scales on her legs itched.

White hair. Blazing blue eyes.

Wisteria swayed, her throat dry, as the marble floor swirled beneath her. ". . . Prim?"

～

Once secured in the man's office, Wisteria felt a tad better. For one thing, without the crowd, she felt like she could breathe better. The young man had also secured a seat for her, an ornate wooden chair pressed against the wall. From there, she could sip the pink punch out of the crystal cup he'd obtained for her and study the room. The wallpaper was pretty, a soft blue color with tiny white-and-gold designs woven in a pattern. Other peculiarities decorated the room, too, things she'd only seen in storybooks or heard tales about from the other girls. So the grandfather clocks *didn't* have carved beards or look like old men—an interesting misnomer, then.

But the most interesting thing in the chamber had to be the stranger standing before her in his white-and-gold doublet. From the way he'd commanded authority over the guards, and the fact he'd taken her to *his* office, she had the niggling suspicion she'd crashed into the prince himself, whose easy-going attitude also didn't fit her expectations. From the stories she'd read as a child, she thought princes were aloof, serious, and perhaps even a bit pretentious. But this stranger smiled and laughed easily, as if they were old friends.

He must have caught her staring, because he cleared his throat. "First, let me introduce myself." He locked his fingers together. "I think it's only fitting you know the name of your target." He grinned, his ivory-colored teeth dazzling against his ebony skin. "I'm Prince Aurelius, but you can call me Ari. I always find introductions help foster that interpersonal assassin-and-target bond."

Wisteria choked on her drink.

Aurelius's—Ari's—smirk deepened. "Ah, so you *do* have a sense of humor. That's good. I'm afraid I'd be disappointed if my murderer was a stick in the mud. Or a stick in the sand, whatever you mermaids prefer." He paused. "I *am* assuming you're a mermaid. I mean, I haven't seen the scales on your legs, but to ask you to flash anything above your ankle might be a little *too* personal."

"Why would you assume I'm a mermaid?" Wisteria's hands tightened on her cup until her knuckles matched the shade of her hair.

"Well, because you said Prim's name earlier on the steps. And you look like her spitting image, except your eyes are golden instead of blue." Ari flashed that dazzling smile at her again.

Oh, *perfect*. Wisteria hadn't been born for the life of an assassin, and she'd certainly never received any of Lady Ambrosia's training. But despite her ineptitude, she hadn't thought she'd expose herself *this* quickly.

Lacking anything intelligent to say, she whispered, "Oh. I'm sorry."

"Don't worry. I won't throw you in prison for being a mermaid *or* for your mission." Ari strolled around the mahogany desk to claim a seat in the matching chair opposite Wisteria. The globe on the desk rattled as he propped his boot up on the edge of the wood and relaxed against the back of his chair. Once settled, he rocked himself back and forth with his toe.

For the first time, Wisteria made eye contact and let her gaze linger. "You know my mission? Then—then shouldn't you have me executed on the spot?"

Ari twisted up his face. "Mm. I can. There are guards who will be in here with a snap of my fingers. Is that what you desire?"

"If I'm to be a prisoner with you or Lady Ambrosia, I think I'd much prefer up here. At least you have decent drinks." Wisteria dropped her attention back to her punch and took another quiet sip. "If you knew Prim, I assume you also have heard of Lady Ambrosia."

"The Sea Witch, yes. Prim mentioned her several times." His voice sounded soft. "She mentioned she was a very cruel mistress."

"And she *liked* Prim, I think. As much as someone with a wicked heart can." Wisteria's lip trembled, and she hastily blinked back tears, but a few still fell before she could catch them. She sniffed. "I'm—I'm sorry. I'd almost beg you to arrest me if I didn't have to go back, but she'd just send a more competent assassin after me. Seems like a rotten deal for you."

Ari's chair paused. A moment lingered. Gently, he whispered, "And what about *you*? You're the one in jail."

Wisteria shrugged. She really *was* the worst assassin, prattling on like this. She didn't know what Lady Ambrosia taught the other girls, but she highly doubted it consisted of chatting with their targets, spoiling their mission within the first hour, and begging to be thrown in jail.

Squeak, squeak, squeak went his chair again. "Please, don't cry. You won't be thrown into the dungeon on my watch. I strictly forbid it."

Wisteria furrowed her brow, raising her eyes once more. "Why? You should. You don't need to be this nice to a mermaid who's supposed to kill you."

"Maybe. But, try as I might, I can't bring myself to fear a girl who's crying into her punch." Ari let his chair drop with a dull *thunk* and lowered his feet. His demeanor shifted as he opened a desk drawer and pulled out a silver, bejeweled dagger. The air no longer felt jovial or friendly; he rose and strode back around the desk with the purpose and meaning of a king. In that moment, it wasn't hard for Wisteria to imagine him ruling a nation and commanding the respect of all who were under him, like the princes in the tales.

He paused, one stride away from her, and held the dagger out to her, hilt first. His expression was grim. "So I'll give you a choice. If you're going to kill me, do it now. To be honest, it would be easier that way. I'm tired of the war and tired of living with my life in constant danger. If you kill me now, you can leave through this window." He gestured to a large window overlooking the thick trees behind the palace. "There are no guards down there tonight. If you run first to the left and then break toward the shoreline once you're a few miles away, you'll escape. I won't scream, won't protest. No one will find you, and your mission will be complete. You'll have your freedom. Lady Ambrosia won't be able to make you cry anymore."

"What?" Wisteria hastily stood, sloshing some punch over the edge of her cup. "Are you *insane*? Why—"

Their noses were only inches from each other's, their eyes locked. Ari held the dagger between them, its blade pointed at his stomach.

One bump could plunge that blade into his flesh, and the thought didn't fill Wisteria with excitement. Rather, her whole body felt tense and panicked.

"Put it down," she whispered. "Please."

The electric moment hung between them as they studied each other's faces, striving to understand each other's intentions.

"You ask me how I can trust you." Ari's voice was low, husky. "Does this answer your question?"

"You're insane." Wisteria swallowed. "You can't just give your enemies prime opportunities to kill you."

"No, but you can be vulnerable with people you want to befriend."

Wisteria's heartbeat reverberated in her ears, almost louder than her voice. "You don't even know me."

"I know the most important thing about you, something I would consider invaluable in a friendship." Ari's gaze held hers. "You won't kill me, even when doing so would come at immense personal gain."

With that, he stepped away, switching his grip on the dagger so that he held the hilt instead of the blade. The stillness of the moment shattered, and Wisteria slumped down into her seat. Her knees felt weak and her whole body jittery. She clenched one fist, the gesture her only outlet for all her pent-up stress, though she really wanted to scream, long and loud.

Ari's smile returned in full force, bright like the sun. He tossed the dagger onto the desk. It skidded over a few papers before it came to rest next to the ornate globe. "There. With all the formalities out of the way, I think it's time we finish introductions. You never gave me your name, but you have to be Prim's sister. Wisteria, right? She called you Wish."

It'd been years since anyone had used that nickname. Tears welled up in Wisteria's eyes again. How odd that the droplets didn't drift away on the ocean currents immediately. "Yes."

Ari's gaze softened, and he leaned down in front of her and took her hand. "I'm sorry for everything you've been through. Prim told me a great deal about you—and what you'd both been through. We shared grief in many ways. My own mother died when I was three, and I've been raised by the crotchety old men and women of the council since. You know the sort—they care mostly about the country and my education, and, as I've recently come of age, whether or not I'm properly wedded so they can pass on the responsibility of the country to me."

"I'm sorry for you, too." Wisteria's hand lingered in Ari's. His touch had been so gentle that she hadn't even flinched. She sniffed, though a few of her tears already dotted her skin. "You've not had it easy."

"Says the girl who's been a slave for most of her life." Ari chuckled. "At least I've had the comforts of a palace and a great many servants who love me."

"But that doesn't negate the fact that you've lost both your parents, too." The words spilled out of Wisteria. "And this awful war that's been raging on, and—"

Ari's loud laughter cut her off again. He wrapped his arms around her in a hug, and she uttered a tiny exclamation of shock, dropping her cup onto the floor. The contents spilled onto the rug as the cup shattered. Ari didn't chide her, though; he merely said, "Thank you."

"For what? Breaking your crystalware?" Wisteria blinked. Her breathing quickened, and she glanced around as if someone might be able to instruct her on how to hug again. As it was, her back tensed, and her arms dangled uselessly at her sides.

"No, for your empathy. You and Prim are quite amazing." Ari squeezed her once before he released her. "Sorry. I didn't mean to make you uncomfortable with a hug."

"Oh, no. It's . . . it's fine. I didn't mind. It's just . . . been a long while. I feel like I've forgotten how." Heat scalded Wisteria's cheeks, and she focused on the broken pieces of the cup on the floor so she wouldn't have to make eye contact. How interesting—three shards of crystal lay at her feet. Three. A nice number, even if it wasn't even.

"Don't worry. I'm an excellent teacher, and I think you'll be a quick study, if you like." Ari bent and picked up the cup without acknowledgment of her clumsiness. "Regardless, Prim spoke highly of you, and now I see all her stories were true." He glanced up once before he returned to his job. "She thought we might have the opportunity to meet one day. Toward the end of her month, when the poison had made it harder for her to walk, she prepared my father and I for what was to come. She worried the Sea Witch might kidnap you to fulfill the family debt." He placed the cup fragments to the side. Pink stained the carpet, but he didn't acknowledge that, either—nor the five . . . six . . . *seven* splatters on the hardwood. "We assumed Prim's sacrifice would buy us more time, but my father was dead within the week. And I've been, in some form or fashion, alone ever since." Ari lifted his gaze to meet hers again, his words soft and tender. "You have no idea how long I've been looking for you."

Wisteria snorted. As if she didn't keep track of numbers for everything in her life. "Ten years, three months, and two days?"

"Ah, well, all right. I suppose you do." Another chuckle slipped past his lips. "I'm very sorry if I accosted you right as you entered the ball. We didn't even get a chance to dance or flirt before we skipped straight to attempted stabbing. I robbed you of the chance with my eagerness to meet you." He shifted his weight again, and a glint on his jacket drew her attention to the buttons there. "But do you think we can be friends?"

Wisteria finished her latest count while he spoke. "You have an even twelve buttons on your coat, so I suppose that's a point in your favor. Frankly, if you'd had eleven, I would have rethought my choice to not stab you."

Ari put a hand over his heart. "As you should."

This time, Wisteria laughed along with him.

"So—if you'll be my friend, I have a proposition," Ari said. "I'd like for you to help me continue Prim's work. End this war once and for all, in her honor."

Wisteria took out one of the starfish pinning her hair in its updo. Loose curls spilled out, and with each tendril she freed, she felt more herself and less Lady Ambrosia's plaything. "I don't know if I can. Lady Ambrosia only gave me three days, and . . . I'm not Prim. She was always braver and smarter than I was."

Ari raised his hand. "If you're going to put yourself down, stop right there." He rose from the floor and moved behind the mahogany desk. For a few seconds, he shuffled papers around before pulling out a yellowed envelope sealed with red ink. "Before she left, Prim gave my father and me this—her plan for the worst, though she hoped for the best." Ari crossed the floor to Wisteria and offered her the envelope. "Her instructions were to give it to you if you ever came to Iylamor. She hoped to bring you here herself, but . . . well, I'm very sorry that never happened."

Wisteria's hand trembled as she reached for the letter. Hidden inside the envelope was the last message her sister ever left for her, her last farewell. Perhaps Prim's apologies for not being able to rescue Wisteria.

She took a deep, steadying breath and held it for exactly ten seconds.

Starving for one scrap of hope, Wisteria tore into the letter.

Dearest Wish,

I don't know how long has passed between me penning these words and you reading them, but I expect you've grown into a beautiful young woman by now. I suspect I won't get to see it happen, though, because I'm going to disobey Ambrosia. Even now, I can feel the poison in my stomach, burning me alive. I doubt I will ever get to see you again, and I am so, so sorry.

But sometimes you have to make hard choices.

I know it seems like we haven't had any say in our lives since Mother and Father fell into Ambrosia's debt. I'd like to think they didn't know or understand the consequences of their actions. It helps me focus on the good memories and not the resentment that might turn me bitter, especially since Father still died and Mother followed soon after. But here we are, slaves to the Sea Witch.

More than likely, you are here to assassinate King Cyrillus. But he and Prince Ari are good people. Friends. They are tired of this senseless war over their border, of being punished for the crime of existing. I have chosen to fight the Sea Witch—but the time has come to make your own choice.

Your choices boil down to this: you may obey Ambrosia, kill your target, and return for the antidote. You will live. You may even earn your freedom.

Or you can try and end this senseless war once and for all. After all . . . women always finish the wars men start. You could use your time here to stop this war, even if you face death because of your disobedience.

It will not be easy. As I write this, my month is almost up. I have failed, but, should you choose to help Cyrillus and Ari, I am leaving you all my research to give you a headstart. I thought siren songs might help stop the war, but I have thus far been unsuccessful in finding a useful one. I believe in you, though.

Iylamor's fate is in your hands—but so is your own.

For once, do what you believe is right. Not what Ambrosia or I tell you.

All I want is for you to be free to choose.

Love,

Prim

Primrose's careful handwriting blurred as Wisteria drank in each precious quill stroke. If someone had offered her a choice between having Ari's entire castle or these short paragraphs written by Primrose's hand, Wisteria would have walked away with her sister's last words. She hugged the pages to her chest as though that might make the words absorb into her skin and bring life to her numb, aching heart.

Ari leaned over her shoulder. He smelled sweet—a scent she couldn't place, but one so far removed from the sea, from Lady Ambrosia, that it felt comforting. "Will you help Iylamor end the war, Wish?"

She sniffled. Death followed every decision, but at least she could decide who would face that death.

"I will," she whispered. "You have my word."

Ari clasped her shoulder. "And you have my word—as a prince and as a friend—I will not let you die. If we fail, you can take my life or I'll go down and get the antidote for you. It only seems fair that we have equal consequences at stake."

"What?" Wisteria whipped around. "No! You can't—why would you—you're a *prince*—"

"So? A title does not give me more worth than you." Ari leaned against the edge of the desk.

"But it's a deep dive! Several meters below Witch Rock—"

"I've done deep dives before. I'm quite skilled."

Wisteria shook her head. "Lady Ambrosia will kill you."

Ari waved her worries away. "If we fail, I may not die by your hand, but I will die. Ambrosia will send another assassin, just like she did with my father."

"So we're both dead." Wisteria sighed.

Then a laugh drew her attention back to Ari, who grinned again. "Isn't that a cheery thought? Anyway, enough chit-chat. Every extra syllable gets us one foot deeper in the grave." He reached for her hand. "Ready to see what we've discovered so far?"

～〰〰～

Ari's library was larger than anything Wisteria had seen under the sea. Tall shelves lined every wall, each one so humongous that anyone other than a giant from a storybook would need one of the room's several ladders to reach the top shelves. A wide window stretched from roof to floor, and moonlight wafted in and cast long shadows.

Wisteria gaped at all these new wonders, but most of all the fireplace opposite the window. She dared not get too close to the grate, but she stood staring, hypnotized by the way the flames danced, until Ari shook her shoulder.

"Look. Here is all our research." Ari turned her around and gestured to a pile on the long rectangular table nearby. Fourteen chairs lined it, six on both sides and one at each of the ends. Everything was equal and neat—

"Wish." Ari shook her gently. "Are you listening?"

She blinked up at him. "Hm? Oh. What did you say?"

His dimples appeared as he smiled, showing no sign of irritation at her distracted counting. "I said, siren songs intrigued Prim. For years, they've been known to start wars or lure people to their deaths. But she wondered if there might be a song that would do the opposite. You know—why do siren songs *have* to be evil?"

Wisteria glanced down at a drawing of a mermaid stretched out on a rock. *Lorelei's Song,* the caption read. She picked up a scrap of paper inked with two fearsome mermaids: *Scylla's Song* under one and *Charybdis's Song* under another.

"I recognize these names." Wisteria tapped the page. "Lady Ambrosia has books about them. Sometimes I heard her teaching the other girls from them."

Ari tilted his head. "What do her books say?"

"Just that their songs would lure people to their deaths. But they don't look like this." Wisteria traced her finger over their tails. "They look terrifying in her books. More monster than mermaid. More like . . ." She swallowed. "Lady Ambrosia."

Ari's eyes lit up, and he tugged another book out of the stack of leather tomes and flipped it open. "Like this, maybe?"

Wisteria bit off a gasp. Even more grotesque than the drawings in Lady Ambrosia's collection, this sketch of Scylla no longer had a tail—only dozens of snakes writhing from various parts of her body. Instead of teeth, fangs filled her mouth, and she had an unearthly pallor to her skin like that of a bloated corpse.

"This one was drawn by the author right before he killed her," Ari said. "Or so the legend goes."

Wisteria turned between the two pictures. One depicted a mermaid maiden, while the other showed a terrifying demon. "So Scylla writes a song, and somehow shifts from this to that." She tapped each rendition in turn. "But what happened in between?"

Ari gestured to the library. "Welcome to what I've been trying to piece together for years. My best guess is that each time a mermaid uses a siren song, she becomes more and more monstrous. I don't know why, but I've spent years trying to figure out if there's a way to circumvent the transformation and use siren songs for good. To end wars, not start them. Give life instead of death."

"And you want me to do it in three days, when you couldn't do it in ten years?" Wisteria asked dryly.

"We're on the brink of a breakthrough. I can feel it." Ari placed a hand over his heart. "Besides, I've done all the research. You just have to pick my brain and put together all the puzzle pieces we have. It's the easiest part, really."

Wisteria rolled her eyes. Oh, to have his unabashed bravado and blind faith. "Won't your guests start to wonder where you are, though? All the eligible maidens down there will be anxious to have their chance at being your wife."

Ari screwed up his face and stuck his tongue out. "All the staff and guards know my plans have changed. They'll enjoy redirecting all those potential brides so we can plot how to save our lives."

Wisteria snorted. "You have a plan for everything, don't you? Guess we better get started, then. We only have until midnight before my legs disappear for the day." She glanced at the grandfather clock in the corner. Four hours and seventeen minutes. "You'd best talk quickly."

Ari flashed a smile. "That's my specialty."

⌁

For nearly four hours, songs and legends danced around Wisteria's brain. It seemed every siren of legend had a special song. Songs for whirlpools, songs for seduction, songs for hypnotizing. But not a single melody seemed conducive to their situation.

She stared mindlessly at the coat of arms above the fireplace, an engraved wrought-iron shield with two gilded swords thrust into it. Sighing, she rubbed her fingers along her temple. The music and laughter drifting up from the ballroom irritated her—she liked to work in perfect silence—but at least Ari had set a guard at the door so that no one disturbed them. "What if we try a song of seduction? It turns men into mindless zombies. Maybe they'll stop fighting."

Ari raised his eyebrows. "Oh? You want thousands of lustful soldiers running after you, then? You didn't exactly strike me as that kind of girl."

Heat flushed Wisteria's face, and she shook her head. "That's not what I meant! I just thought it would make them forget about the battle. Which—what if I hypnotize the whole army instead? They'll stop fighting if I tell them to. That's the same principle, but without the lust."

The grandfather clock ticked loudly in the background, reminding them of the deepening night, and Ari yawned. "Can you hypnotize the whole Briglen army at once? I've only read of a siren affecting a few people at most."

"I . . . don't know. Lady Ambrosia didn't teach me anything. But she's got a lot of books in her grotto." Oddly, Wisteria had never counted all the tomes in Lady Ambrosia's library, so she didn't have an exact tally of what was there. "Maybe when I go back tonight I can look."

"Will she be mad if she catches you? It doesn't seem like it takes a lot for her to resort to murder."

Wisteria swallowed. The poison churned inside her, and she put a fist against her middle to steady herself. "I'm a dead girl in two days anyway." Forty-eight hours and twenty minutes until her midnight deadline, to be exact.

"I told you. I'm not letting you die. Neither one of us is dying." Ari's eyes flickered to her fist. "What's wrong?"

"The poison." Wisteria flinched as the brew churned inside her, filling her with fire. If it didn't lessen soon, she might throw up. "It's nothing."

Ari scowled. "Maybe I should just go get you the antidote and be done with this ridiculous time limit."

"And how do you expect to get there or fight underwater? Surrounded by assassins who will kill you with one word from her? Lady Ambrosia is dangerous in her own right; the only reason she doesn't kill men herself is because she won't come on land." After all, why *would* the Sea Witch subject herself to pain and poison when she could inflict it upon girls in her debt?

Ari grumbled and leaned back in his seat, his boots propped up on the table. Worst-case scenarios danced through Wisteria's mind, and they made her want to reach out and grab him before anything bad could happen. Like him tilting back too far and crashing to the floor, snapping his neck—

"Fine, I won't go after her . . . for now. But you'll be back tomorrow, right?" Ari's voice broke her out of her anxious reverie.

"I'll be back until we're both dead," Wisteria replied. And, just to seal it . . . She shifted in her seat so Ari couldn't see her hand as it drifted up her thigh.

There. She could feel a few scales hiding beneath the layers of her dress. She squeezed her eyes shut and yanked one free.

Even with the warning, she still sucked in a breath of pain as the scale broke free of her skin. She rubbed the tender spot with the heel of her palm and waited for the throbbing to recede before she swiveled around to face Ari again.

"Here." She dropped the black-and-gold scale into his hand.

"A scale?" Ari curled his fingers around it and smiled. "Thank you, Wish. I've read about these. They're quite meaningful—a bit of mermaid's magic still resides in them."

"Yes, but they're important for more than just their magical properties. Mermaids exchange them with solemn vows." Wisteria rested her hand over his closed fingers. "I promise, on this very scale, I will be back tomorrow."

"And I promise, on this very scale, I will be waiting for you." A slow smile spread across his face, and he offered her a wink. "I shall not let any other assassin stab me without your explicit permission."

They bid each other goodbye, and Wisteria exited the library, pushing her way through the throng of dancers in the ballroom. The stifling air choked her—so many humans, so little space, even in a grand castle. If only she could run, get free from this suffocating atmosphere, but she could hardly even *walk*, let alone move any quicker.

Pain spread throughout her body again, but nowhere worse than in her feet; it felt like knives jabbing her with every step as she escaped the palace.

At the shoreline, she gladly kicked off the dreaded sea glass slippers and stumbled into the foam just as the clock in the castle tower pealed. Wisteria felt each gong reverberate inside her chest, from one to twelve, while the transformation magic swelled inside her. Closing her eyes, she succumbed to the spell, letting it shift her back into a mermaid.

She fell face-first into the waves and almost kissed them in relief.

Mermaids simply weren't made to walk on two feet. And that was no more apparent than when she wiggled out of her dress and turned around to grab her shoes so no one could steal them.

Blood stained the bottom of the sea glass slippers.

<p style="text-align:center">~~~~~</p>

Notes and lyrics filled Wisteria's gaze as she flipped through the weathered seaweed pages of *The Mermaid Hymnal*, the biggest book in Lady Ambrosia's library. This book housed every song she'd read about with Ari earlier in the night, plus more. Songs to poison. Songs to kill. Songs of death, destruction, and tragedy.

Two hundred and five of them, and not a single one could save Iylamor.

Poison churned inside her stomach. Pain seized her and she dropped to the cavern floor, one hand clinging to the podium where she'd propped up the hymnal. Wisteria gasped, squeezing her eyes closed.

Numbers swirled in her head—time ticked forward, ever closer to the deadline. If she died, Ari would, too, and his kingdom would fall.

She couldn't sleep, no matter how much exhaustion toyed with her. Couldn't stop. She needed a song of peace, a song of something *nice* . . .

Maybe she could write it. Even though she wasn't educated about siren songs, perhaps learning would be easy enough.

Or maybe she'd end up an ugly monster like the ones in Ari's books, but an ugly monster was still a *living* one.

She sucked in a breath and opened her mouth to let the first few quiet notes trail out. *I want . . . I want peace,* she whispered in her mind, to pour her intentions into the notes. A tingling feeling crept down her spine, and she shivered. Her voice cracked with a painful snap that felt like something had bit the inside of her throat.

A tentacle wrapped around Wisteria's waist.

She shrieked, her song cutting off, as Lady Ambrosia hoisted her upwards. Wisteria flapped her tail and punched at Lady Ambrosia's grasp, but that only made the pressure tighten on her midsection.

"Fighting back? That's not like you, Wisteria." Lady Ambrosia slithered out of the shadows. The glow stones cast eerie reflections on her round face. "What were you singing?"

"I—I . . ." Wisteria swallowed. Too many excuses caught inside her throat until a half-truth spilled out. "I want to write my own song. To . . . kill Ar—the prince. I'll sing it at the ball, and . . ." Her mind stalled, unable to formulate anything else.

"No need. You have the knife, don't you?" Lady Ambrosia drew Wisteria closer. Another tentacle curled around Wisteria's fluke. Visions of being torn apart flickered through her head and she squirmed more. Her heartbeat sped up, and a burst of panic fluttered to life inside her chest.

"But—I'm a mermaid. I want to sing. I want . . ." A third of Lady Ambrosia's tentacles snaked around Wisteria's throat.

"Don't get a smart head, Wisteria," Lady Ambrosia hissed. "Don't think you can cheat your fate. You are *mine*, and you will do as I say."

Wisteria gagged. If she held her breath, could she survive? The pressure grew tighter, tighter, *tighter*, strangling the life from her.

"You want to sing? Go ahead and give it a try." Lady Ambrosia chuckled. "Here's what no one told me, *dearie*. When a siren sings, she has to give up part of herself. I used to be like you, with a pretty little tail. But the more I sang, the more I lost." A dark smile flickered across Lady Ambrosia's face. "The sirens of old lost much in pursuit of power. My own mistress lost her life when she got a little too ambitious and tried to turn a whole country into seafoam. So go ahead and sing. If you're trying to kill someone, *you* will die trying."

Spots danced in Wisteria's vision until Lady Ambrosia released her. Wisteria gasped, her hands going to her neck as she sank to the floor. Her eyes burned, and she struggled to contain all the pent-up emotions.

But what if I'm trying to help someone? The silent question died on Wisteria's tongue, joined by many others. *Can someone write a siren song for good? Can I help people with my voice? I don't care about power. I would give up anything to finish Prim's mission and save Ari. I just want to help him stop this war. Help him stop you.*

"Don't you dare try and double-cross me like your sister did." Lady Ambrosia grasped Wisteria's white hair and dragged her out of the room. Wisteria pinched her eyes shut and bit her tongue so she wouldn't cry out and garner more of the Sea Witch's wrath. "Stab the boy and be done with it. But if I find you betrayed me, I'll kill you just like I killed her."

The poison in Wisteria's stomach grew hotter, like a cauldron set to boil. She wanted to defend Prim's memory, her honor. But all she could do was gasp for air, pulling at her hair in an attempt to free herself.

Lady Ambrosia towed Wisteria deeper into the grotto, past the cavern recesses that acted as bedrooms for the other girls. At the very back of the cave, the Sea Witch slung Wisteria into the room that had acted as her prison for ten years.

Wisteria couldn't be stuck there for another decade. Not when Ari's survival hinged on her helping him. "Not—not a traitor." Wisteria clutched her sore throat and glared up at Lady Ambrosia from the floor, but the Sea Witch seemed unbothered by the vitriol in Wisteria's gaze. "I want to *prove* . . ." Wisteria coughed. ". . . *prove* . . . self . . . not weak."

"Meter your ambition, chit," Lady Ambrosia snarled. "Remember that my poison will kill you in a few days, but *I* can end your life at any time." One tentacle shoved Wisteria further into the darkness of her chamber. "Kill the boy. Your life and freedom hang in the balance."

〜〜〜

If Wisteria had hoped to avoid any questions about what Ambrosia had done, she failed the moment she entered Ari's library the next day. The servant who had escorted her up closed the door after her, and she found Ari seated at the table.

He leapt up when she entered, a wide grin on his face. But his expression fell when their eyes met, and he rushed forward. "What happened?" When he reached for her neck, she flinched, though his touch was far more gentle than the Sea Witch's.

"Lady Ambrosia," Wisteria whispered hoarsely. Her eyes dropped. "She caught me snooping."

"She bruised you." Ari tugged her into his arms—but again, unlike the Sea Witch, the gesture was tender.

Wisteria sniffed and rested her head against his chest. They shouldn't do this, not when they had work to do, but she'd been deprived of a steady source of hugs for so long. She hadn't had someone be so affectionate since Prim was alive—over ten years ago.

Ten years since Wisteria had a friend.

"Was she trying to stop you from singing?" Ari asked sharply. "Did you find the song?"

Wisteria shook her head. "No. I tried to write my own."

"Do you think that would work? If you could write your own song . . ."

"She said I'd die if I sang." Some part of Wisteria felt weak for even admitting it, especially because she had the suspicion Ari would refuse to let her sing if he knew the consequences.

Just as she predicted, he whispered, "So we'll find another way." He gave her a squeeze. "And if not, how do you feel about being tomb-mates, buried together?"

Despite the gravity of the situation—or perhaps because of it—a laugh burst out of Wisteria.

"There we go. There's a laugh. See? It'll be all right, no matter what. Though I confess, at the end of the day, I'd like to survive." Ari released her after another thorough once-over. "Besides. She could be lying. That snake would say anything to try and keep her reputation."

"I don't know." Wisteria rubbed her throat, which still ached from the night before.

Ari started to pace in front of the nearest bookcase. He traversed the whole shelf, pivoted, and turned back, only to repeat the cycle. Wisteria could appreciate the repetitive actions.

On his third trip, he paused right by a ladder. "Why don't we try it?"

Wisteria walked over to a chair by the table and sat down, wincing as she slid out of her shoes. At least no fresh blood had sullied them yet today. "Try what?"

"Try singing. One time. A song that you write for peace."

Such a simple suggestion, and something that Prim would do. Last night's failure wouldn't have mattered. Prim would have tried it again, if only to defy Lady Ambrosia. But that was typical for Prim. She'd always been the feisty one, the one who charged at bullies with calculated fury, the one who had always been three lengths ahead in everything. If anyone could have bested Lady Ambrosia, it should have been Prim.

"I tried. Last night. And . . . it didn't work."

Ari marched over to her and claimed her hands. He drew her out of her seat and ushered her to the center of the room as if she was a performer on a stage. "But you didn't die, so that proves that Lady Ambrosia has to be lying, right? Please, Wish. Try once more. I believe in you. Maybe that's the magic. You just need one person in the room who thinks you're capable of doing miracles."

She wanted to roll her eyes. To cower in fear, to say life didn't work that way. But for so long, she'd suffered under the abusive thumb of Lady Ambrosia, and now this prince offered her a smidgen of hope.

His fingers paused, then he tucked a strand of hair behind her ear. Before she knew it, he cupped her cheek and brought their foreheads together. "I won't make you sing if you really don't want to. But I believe in you—with every fiber of my being. We're close, Wish. We're close to accomplishing everything Prim and my father believed we could."

Wisteria's cheeks flamed underneath his fingers. His other arm wrapped around her back, and she didn't think she could *breathe*, let alone sing. Yet, somehow, she also felt like she could do *everything* now, if only he didn't move. If he stayed there to help her.

She closed her eyes. Steeled her insides. Opened her mouth.

She infused all her thoughts, hopes, wishes, and prayers into the first few notes. Into the peace, the comfort she wanted to bring. Ari exhaled softly, his breath a small breeze against her. He closed his eyes, his thumb tracing her cheek—

Her throat seized up, and the fourth note soured.

She coughed, her knees buckling. If not for Ari, she would have fallen, but his grip tightened around her, pinning her against his chest so they sank to the floor in a controlled manner.

The poison roiled inside of her, as angry as the sea in a hurricane. "Wish? Wish, what's wrong?"

"My voice." It cracked even as she uttered the words. She sounded more like a frog than a girl. She had to clear her throat roughly several times before she could speak again. "It hurts." She coughed; when she spoke next, her voice was hoarse. "I can't. I'm not doing it right. I don't—I don't know *how* to do it."

"Okay." Ari brought her head against his chest. His hand rested on the nape of her neck, a secure, warm presence. "I'm sorry. Don't try it again. We'll figure something out, all right?"

Wisteria squeezed her eyes shut so he wouldn't see her cry. "I'm sorry, too. I'm sorry I'm not Prim. She could do it. She could do anything."

"Don't you apologize for being yourself." Ari sighed, and his breath tickled her scalp.

"But . . . I'm so weak compared to her."

He let out a low snort. "You are anything but. Do you think someone weak could walk into their death knowingly? Do you think someone weak would risk everything for the sake of another? You are not weak, Wish. Not in the slightest."

"I can't sing, though. I can't do the one thing you need me to do." Wisteria sagged against him. Her eyes burned, her muscles were sore, and her insides were scorched.

"Then we'll find a different way." Ari rubbed at the back of her head gently. "I'll keep working. You rest. If you were in the grotto trying to find a book all night, I doubt you slept."

Wisteria shook her head, her tongue too heavy to talk at the moment.

"Then go to sleep." Ari adjusted his grip so her head could rest more easily against his chest. "I'll keep searching. There's just one puzzle piece we haven't found, Wish. And when we find it, it will make everything better. But we're not going to be able to do it if you're exhausted." His voice was low and soft, almost like a lullaby. "Rest now. I'll keep you safe."

With a last sigh, and wrapped in a warm, tender embrace, Wisteria gave herself over to exhaustion.

~~~~~

The sun painted the horizon brilliant hues of pink, orange, and yellow as it rose beyond the line of the sea.

What a beautiful day to die.

Wisteria pulled herself from the ocean. She could feel Lady Ambrosia's steely gaze on her back. The sea glass dagger thrummed against Wisteria's side, reminding her that this was the third and final
~~~~~

day. These were the last few hours she had to kill Ari, to betray the only person who had been nice to her in ten years—the first *friend* she'd had in a very long time. All the other girls in the grotto had kept their distance, afraid to create any bonds that could be used against them. And in the end, that would be exactly what happened to Wisteria. Her bond with Ari would kill one of them, *today*.

Pulling on her ballgown once more, Wisteria trudged into the palace. Guards escorted her to the library, and Wisteria counted steps as they walked, a way to distract herself from her raw, sore feet and the burning headache. She needed two steps for each marble square, and there were one-hundred-and-four squares leading to the library door.

Ari—already put together and polished despite the early hour—looked up from his chair as she entered and offered her a solemn nod. "Morning, Wish." He waved at the soldiers, who stepped back and closed the door, leaving the two of them alone. "Did you have any run-ins with Ambrosia last night?"

"No more than usual, but I didn't try to sneak into her library." Wisteria's voice had returned in its full power, but she couldn't walk without limping. She hobbled over to her seat, which Ari pulled away from the table and helped her ease into.

Ari pressed the back of his hand against her forehead. "You feel feverish."

Wisteria blinked slowly. Her mind trudged along, scarcely able to piece together a coherent thought. "This is my last day. I'll die at midnight." Every part of her felt hot, though Ari's cool touch helped some.

"No, you won't. We have today to think of something."

"We have less than seventeen hours to think of something." Wisteria moaned and covered her face. "It's not possible. You've searched for years. We aren't going to find a pre-written song used for good. Every famous siren has used their songs to murder, and it's transformed them into hideous beasts—or killed them. Then the legends about them get darker and more macabre. The songs corrupt all mers who use them."

Indignation bubbled up inside of Wisteria until she wanted to scream. Why did evil have to be so powerful in the world? Why did everyone have to seek power, money, and their own self-interest, to the point that they destroyed every speck of goodness?

The grandfather clock ticked away in the corner of the room. *One, two, three, four, five* . . . No—it wasn't working. Instead of calming her, she could only think of each passing moment as one less she and Ari had to live.

Shuddering, Wisteria dug her fingernails into her temple as if she could stop the pain inside by inflicting pain on the outside. "Not to mention that I can't even *sing*. And if I could, if I tried to kill all your enemies with a powerful song, who's to say I won't just transform into a soulless beast who needs to be murdered?"

"Because . . . you're you." Ari toyed with the edge of one of the many books splayed across the table. All their information, the hundreds of books, lay open to various pages. "You're sweet and kind and—"

"Doomed." With a wince, Wisteria slipped off her sea glass slippers. Part of her wanted to throw them into the fire as one final act of rebellion. "And for all we know, Scylla and even Lady Ambrosia might have been wonderful mermaids before they used their siren songs."

"I don't believe they could ever be like you. Evil people want evil things from the start, Wish. But not you. Prim said—"

"I don't care what Prim said!" Wisteria hadn't meant to yell—but the words had slipped out of her with all the fury of the poisonous fire burning inside her. "I'm not Prim. And maybe I didn't kill you when I had the chance, but I'm not whoever you think I am either. I'm not the girl from whatever stories Prim told you, and I'm *not* Prim."

The grandfather clock ticked and tocked, but Ari didn't speak.

"I'm sorry." Tears bubbled up in her eyes and, once again, the ocean didn't wipe them away.

Ari did. "I'm sorry." He held her chin in his hands. "I don't know what you know about Prim's time here, but it meant more to me than . . . anything. I was a lonely child, shuffled from tutor to tutor. Iylamor is a newer nation, without strong ties, and nobody wanted to send their children to play with me when doing so might incite the wrath of

Briglen." His dark eyes searched her face. "I didn't remember my mother very well, and I had no siblings to play with. Father was the only family I knew. Then Prim came with the news that he was marked for death. But Prim gave me something I hadn't felt in a very long time—hope. And whenever we weren't working on this, she played with me, told me stories. All about you and your family, and . . ." He sighed, his gaze dropping from hers. "I'm sorry if I've put too many expectations on you. But you haven't disappointed me, not once. Maybe I've had a slim lot to choose from, but . . . I've never had better friends than you and Prim, Wish. Not because of the time you've devoted for me, but because you've both fought beside me. You've given me hope in ways I didn't think possible."

More tears rolled down Wisteria's face, but Ari caught every one of them with his thumbs. And when he started to cry, too, she reached up and brushed his tears away.

"I understand lonely childhoods better than most," Wisteria said. "When I was little, my father grew very ill. The doctors couldn't do anything for him, so my mother turned to the Sea Witch. She thought Lady Ambrosia could offer some sort of healing, but . . . the Sea Witch's magic always comes with a cost. Father got well, but in return, Lady Ambrosia wanted Prim to become her slave." The memories, long locked behind closed doors in Wisteria's consciousness, started to leak out through the cracks of her mind. She held onto Ari tighter. His steady arms kept her afloat as the tides of her tumultuous, repressed emotions rushed out, threatening to drown her. "My parents refused. They hadn't been told the price would be that high. But it didn't matter in the end. Father fell sick again, and Mother soon after. When there was no one left to protest, Lady Ambrosia swooped in, took Prim as her slave, and I was delivered to the orphanage, I suppose until I could be of better use to her."

And even the worst days at the orphanage had felt like bliss compared to what Wisteria endured when Lady Ambrosia kidnapped her, demanding her life for Prim's failure.

Every brutal year since then, Wisteria had been nothing but an example to the other girls of what would happen if they betrayed Lady Ambrosia. That if they dared defy her, their loved ones would be taken as prisoners, ignored and isolated, without hope of freedom. And not a single girl had stepped a fin out of line or showed Wisteria a bit of kindness, lest they garner the Sea Witch's wrath.

Ari's forehead creased. "That wasn't fair."

Wisteria snorted. "You really expected the Sea Witch to play *fair*?"

Ari pressed his lips against her feverish forehead. "Then we won't either. We'll think of something. But . . ." He sucked in a deep, shaky breath. "If we fail . . . you can stab me and be done with it. I refuse to let you die for me."

Wisteria's head felt light, as if it didn't exist on her shoulders. Her mind couldn't function past the moment they'd just shared, and she didn't think it was due to the poison in her veins. Rather, she blamed the over-zealous butterflies inside her stomach. "I'm *not* going to kill you, Ari. It's my family's debt. My parents' naive mistake. My price to pay."

"It's not. If we place blame on anyone, we assign it to the monster who caused all this." He pulled away and cleared his throat. "It's no more your fault than it is mine that I'm marked for death."

Except one of them could escape their fate, when it came down to it.

"No, no. Listen." Wisteria sat up a bit straighter, and who knew if the crazed look she could feel twisting across her face came from her idea or her temperature. "You need to run away. Forget Iylamor and save your life. If Lady Ambrosia can't find you, then I'm the only one who will die tonight."

"You're asking me to abandon my people? To abandon *you*?" He gaped at her, his eyebrows furrowed.

"I don't know what else you want!" Wisteria gestured to the books behind her, spine after useless spine. "We've tried everything. You've had *years*. Every siren song ever created has led to death." Her breathing hitched, and she grasped her chest as a burst of fire pulsed from her insides. "It can't be done. I want to spend my last day making sure you're safe."

"So you're just going to give up?" Ari grasped her shoulders. "I won't. Not after so long. Everything Prim and my father did, everything I've done, everything *you* did . . . it can't be in vain."

"It won't be! This was never about saving me or Prim. This is about saving *you*." Wisteria touched his cheek, but only for a moment. "As my *friend*, Ari, please. Give me this one choice. Ambrosia has taken away my choice, my *voice*, every day of my life. If the only choice I can ever make is whether or not I live or die on my own terms—I won't let her take that from me. *I* will choose when I die, and for what cause."

Ari rose to his feet, striding over to the fireplace, where he stood with one arm braced on the mantle. "You can make your choices," he said as he stared at the flames. "I won't stop you. You don't have to look in another book for a siren song."

"I'm sorry. It's—it's for the best." Wisteria wrapped her arms around herself. "We'll get you out of Iylamor, somewhere Lady Ambrosia can't reach."

"I can't do that." Ari lifted his head, and their eyes locked. "I won't abandon my people to face Briglen's invaders. I won't leave my friend behind to die in my stead."

Wisteria rubbed her forehead. "You can if the friend is telling you to go."

The flames crackled.

Ari undid the gilded buttons on his golden vest and tossed it on the floor. He loosened the ties on his puffy, fancy shirt next, though he didn't take it off. "And my friend has made her choice. But I can make mine, too."

Wisteria's heart thudded. "What—"

"I'm going to get that antidote for you. Then you won't have to go back in the water. If the Sea Witch doesn't play fair, neither will we. We'll break her blasted time limit." He snatched one of the two swords from its place under the decorative shield that hung above the fireplace.

Wisteria bunched up the fabric of her skirts, her eyes widening. "And how do you think you're going to breathe underwater? You can't hold your breath all the way down from Witch Rock to her lair!"

Ari reached into his pocket. Though she couldn't see what he had inside, she had a sinking feeling she knew what it was.

The prince lifted his chin. "You vowed over this scale that you would come back and help me. Now I'm vowing that I will help *you*."

"Ari, *stop*!" Wisteria cried, but he'd already eaten it before she could rise from her seat.

He shuddered but must have managed to choke the scale down, because he said, "I'll be back with the antidote, Wish. I swear it." With the magic from the scale, he wouldn't have to worry about breathing underwater—he'd soon have his own temporary set of gills.

"No, Ari, wait—" Wisteria stood, but the prince had at least two decades of walking experience on her, and Wisteria had never learned to run. Ari had darted out of the room before she'd even climbed to her feet. Still, she limped after him, leaving bloodied footprints behind.

At the top of the grand staircase, Wisteria grasped the railing and struggled down the steps, but her hurried pace was too much to handle. Her wet, sticky foot slipped, and her bottom slammed against the marble. The blow hurt far worse than it would have underwater. She bit her lip and squeezed her eyes shut to hold back the tears.

All the while, one thought burned through her mind, blazing like the poisonous inferno consuming her body.

Ari was going to die.

It wouldn't matter that she hadn't stabbed him. If he entered the water, the Sea Witch would kill him herself.

⌇⌇⌇

By the time Wisteria reached the shoreline, every part of her ached. She'd left a bloodstained path in her wake, an easy target to follow should any guard she'd passed desire to follow her. They would be no help, though. Not unless they could breathe underwater, and she didn't have enough scales left to give a whole army that ability.

Seashells dug into her feet as she approached the ocean. She winced with every step, pursing her lips so she didn't cry. Ari was nowhere to be seen. Only his boots lingered by the shore, the tide washed against their toes. The boots, empty but upright, gave the illusion of a ghost standing there, invisible in the morning sun.

Less than sixteen hours until her death. Who knew how long until Ari's. What trick would save them now? Holding her breath and counting backward from one hundred? She knew how ridiculous that was, even as her brain longed to latch onto the ritual as a child might cling to a parent for safety.

Wisteria could only think of one option. Leaning down, she touched her fingers to her lips, kissed them, and placed them against the shoes.

Ari would be safe. She'd done the ritual, protected him.

But then again, none of her rituals seemed to be working as of late.

Fear crowded her mind and shortened her breaths, but she had no time to listen to it. Inhaling deeply, Wisteria waded into the water. The waves broke around her long skirts and weighed her down. That would never do. She had to swim quickly to reach Ari.

Wisteria hauled up her skirts to pluck another scale from her thigh so she could eat it. But as she freed the glittering scale, she glimpsed something else.

The sea glass dagger, polished and carved to a point.

Of course—she'd grown so accustomed to its weight that she'd almost forgotten its existence. With a surge of hope, Wisteria stuffed the scale into her mouth and crunched it while she sliced through the bulk of her dress, cutting everything below her knees away. She only kept enough of the skirt to hide the dagger beneath the fabric's voluminous folds. After all, she didn't want to rush into battle unarmed.

There. With the scale, she'd be able to breathe. With her legs freed, she'd be able to swim. With the knife, she'd be able to fight.

She breathed one last sigh before she dove underneath the waves. This time, she faced the unforgiving ocean with legs, not a tail. Her one advantage over the water had been stripped away from her, and she felt as naked as she'd been that first day on Witch Rock.

Hopefully, her legs would be good enough to get her to Lady Ambrosia's lair.

The water darkened around her as the sunlight drained away. Bubbles further impeded her vision, but the scale had worked. Though her sight wasn't as keen as when she had her full powers, the scale's magic helped her see as she traveled down.

She even glimpsed the blood that marred the water around the mouth of Lady Ambrosia's grotto.

Her heart pounded. *Red* blood tinged the water. Not the emerald blood of a mermaid.

Just inside the cavern, the Sea Witch floated with Ari wrapped in four tentacles. He struggled weakly with his sword as blood gushed from a wound on his arm, his face swollen and battered.

But in one hand, he clutched the antidote.

Wisteria didn't think before she screamed.

Lady Ambrosia whipped around. "Somehow, I doubt you brought this little boy down here as a sacrifice. You and sister are so alike that way—always trying to keep this morsel out of my reach."

"Wish," Ari croaked. He sighed, and the sword and vial slipped from his grasp.

Maybe that had been his last word, or maybe he'd been trying to draw her attention to him, the antidote, or the weapon.

But only one appealed to her at that moment.

Wisteria ducked as one tentacle shot toward her and another toward the sword. If Lady Ambrosia managed to get the weapon, Wisteria's paltry dagger would never suffice. So down toward the floor of the grotto Wisteria went, hand outstretched, her fingers barely brushing against the hilt, and—a tentacle coiled around her stomach and jerked her upwards. But it was too late.

She'd grabbed the sword.

"Let him *go*, you witch!" Wisteria screamed, her teeth bared. She hacked at the tentacle that held her hostage, severing it. Lady Ambrosia howled as emerald blood filled the grotto, and her grip slackened on Ari enough for Wisteria to snatch him up and *swim*.

She only had one thought: get to the surface. If she could climb onto Witch Rock, if Lady Ambrosia didn't pursue, Ari might have a chance to live.

Wisteria pumped her legs. Behind her echoed the *whoosh* of displaced water as Lady Ambrosia took off after her. But Wisteria couldn't turn around to check. She had to stay focused on the surface. For herself, for Ari.

With a gasp, Wisteria popped out of the waves near Witch Rock, where this whole mess had begun. Where cruel people like the rulers of Briglen left assassination requests for Lady Ambrosia. And, if their price was right, the heartless Sea Witch murdered indiscriminately for inordinate amounts of wealth and fame.

But here, on this rock of death, Wisteria saw her one shot at living. She tossed the sword onto the rock and, with her fading strength, hauled Ari up after it. Desperate to find some traction, she dug her fingernails into the ground until she bled.

Lady Ambrosia rose from the depths behind them, and a tentacle snaked around Wisteria's neck. She shrieked and writhed as the Sea Witch hoisted her into the air, dangling her above the rock's craggy surface. Another tentacle snatched Ari's sword from where it lay and chucked it far into the waves while a third grabbed the prince himself.

Wisteria's legs thrashed uselessly. The Sea Witch cackled. "Isn't this an absolute *treat*! I get to kill you *and* your audacious prince myself."

"He . . . he doesn't . . . deserve to die," Wisteria choked out. Her breath wouldn't come. Desperation rose like the tide inside her and threatened to strangle her from the inside as the Sea Witch finished the job on the outside. No—it couldn't end like this. Wisteria dug her fingernails into Lady Ambrosia's tentacles, but the Sea Witch didn't flinch, not even when Wisteria tore gashes into the slick skin.

"Isn't it ironic? That's what your sister said about his father." Lady Ambrosia scoffed. She twirled Ari in midair, inspecting him like a shark would inspect a fish. "You're exactly like your brat of a sister." A smile twisted her face.

Dread bubbled in Wisteria's stomach; she'd seen that expression far too many times. A self-satisfied, sadistic smirk. Time must have sped up, because even as the apprehension filled her bones, Wisteria couldn't move fast enough. She couldn't do anything to stop Lady Ambrosia from slinging the unconscious Ari against the tallest point of Witch Rock; he slammed into it and thudded to the ground. Blood trickled down his brow, thick and dark.

Ari! Wisteria stretched out one hand, a futile gesture. A strangled croak escaped her lips, and the edges of her vision turned black.

Lady Ambrosia drew Wisteria closer. "I told Briglen to attack the castle at the stroke of midnight, killing anyone they found inside. What a glorious way to end the prince's little ball, don't you think? Then, with the prince dead and no heir apparent, Iylamor will be in disarray. I do not intend to break my word." Lady Ambrosia smiled that sickening smile again. "You know, I must thank you. Seeing you suffer, scheme, and fail has been such a delight. After the joy you've recently given me, I almost wish the other girls would double-cross me so I could make examples out of *their* weak little sisters."

No.

Lady Ambrosia was wrong.

Wisteria was more than just an *example*.

Ari had believed in her, believed in what she could be.

Wisteria's oxygen supply dwindled, her sight almost gone. But that was all right. She'd played this game before; it was nothing more than a ritual. All Wisteria had to do was hold her breath. She could do it. If she could make it without air for a little while longer, everything would be fine.

She wouldn't let herself or Ari die today.

After all, Lady Ambrosia might have stripped Wisteria of Ari's sword, but she hadn't taken everything.

The sea glass dagger.

Wisteria reached for the dagger hidden underneath her dress. Counting to ten—Wisteria dared not take the time to count higher—she whipped out the weapon and drove it up into the tentacle around her neck.

Lady Ambrosia shrieked. "You little—" Her insult was cut short by another stab. Blackish-green blood splattered onto the rock. Quick as a sailfish—and with just as much deadly intent—Wisteria jammed her dagger into Lady Ambrosia's eye and twisted. The Sea Witch howled, a horrid sound that echoed through the air, and her tentacles seized and released.

Wisteria collapsed against the rocks, gasping for air. Through a fit of hoarse coughing, Wisteria scrambled over to Ari. Rocks dug into her body, and her stomach burned like it might consume her alive. Another worry: the Sea Witch had disappeared under the waves, which meant Wisteria had no idea if her former captor lived or if that awful yowl had been her death cry.

Despite her uncertainty, she had no time to delay. If she didn't get Ari across the small inlet to the shoreline, where the castle with all its guards and doctors waited, *nothing* would matter.

"Come on, Ari." She grunted, wrapping her arms around his torso. "Stay with me, please. *Please.*" Tears rolled down her face, and she choked on her breaking words. With a few more heavy steps, she managed to collapse into the ocean, grateful that the scale's magic still gave her air, because she took a deep breath before they bobbed back up to the surface.

She gave a few measly kicks. Her arms strained, and she grasped Ari's shirt tightly, terrified her strength might give out on her. But she couldn't stop. She had to swim faster. If she hadn't killed Lady Ambrosia, merely blinded her, the Sea Witch would pursue them.

"Come on. We're almost there. We—I—we can do it." On the horizon she could see the tips of the palace towers as they rose into the sky, aglow with brilliant flames of sunlight.

Waves crested over her; with each kick, she spat out seawater. Her heart thudded wildly from exertion, and Ari's limp form offered no help. But she would make it. She *would*.

She'd come too far to die now.

The water became shallower, and she hauled the unconscious prince onto the sand. Her arms trembled as she pulled him off the beach, lugging him toward his home. The palace steps—all twenty-nine of them—became their refuge. She collapsed there, wheezing as all the adrenaline drained from her body.

"Help!" she cried. "Help, *please*!"

Heavy footsteps raced toward her. A peal went up from the bell inside one of the towers. Cries of, "The prince!" flew all around as guards descended upon herself and Ari.

Despite the guards' efforts to pry the two of them apart, Wisteria clung to Ari, while one knight barked at those behind him to fetch the doctors. Carefully, she cradled Ari's head and touched his beaten face. "Ari," she choked out, her voice raw and tender. "Please. Please wake up."

He didn't stir.

"No. No, please. It can't end like this." Each word was a struggle, barely louder than a whisper. Her voice cracked on the last syllable, and tears welled up in Wisteria's eyes. She caressed his cheek, hysteria mounting inside of her. Her mind struggled to do the math—how long had he been underwater? How long had he been bleeding? How long, how long, *how long*?

She cradled his injured arm, begged, pleaded, and sobbed. Someone tried to shove her away, but she squawked at them like a madwoman.

"Come *back*!" she croaked when nothing else worked. "Ari, please! I don't want this! *I don't want this*!"

She could almost hear his teasing voice in her head, as if this whole ordeal was merely another discussion in the library: *then how can you choose differently?*

She didn't have a choice. She couldn't fight death. The only siren songs that existed *caused* death, and she'd failed at writing her own.

Or . . .

Maybe she'd held herself back. Gotten scared by the pain, by the horrible monsters that Lady Ambrosia, Scylla, and Charybdis had become. But with Ari's life on the line . . . did she really want to let fear define her choices?

Wisteria had lived in fear for ten years. She'd depended on rituals and numbers and cowered in the darkness with no hope for the future, no choice in the direction of her life. But the girl who had stabbed the Sea Witch in the eye could also find the courage to lift her voice for her friend.

Wisteria opened her mouth and called upon every mermaid ancestor, every siren—whoever cared enough to listen to a young girl's pleas.

I will give everything I have for a song of life, she thought. *A song of healing. Wisteria's Song. Anything.*

My tail, my voice—anything.

Even my life.

Her lips parted.

With her own pain shoved to the back of her mind, Wisteria's melody soared, louder than any human singer could achieve, but softer still. Sweeter. Filled with memories of Primrose's love, their parents' care, of Ari's hugs and friendly whispers. Wisteria's mind drifted to their time in the library. Funny—she'd never gotten to dance with him at his ball, not once.

She tried to imagine what dancing with him in that magnificent ballroom would have been like and used the sweet daydream to strengthen her song. Her fingers trembled, and she winced as a burst of pain managed to slip past her mental blocks. She would not fall prey to her own injuries or discomfort, not when she had something much bigger to accomplish.

How far away were the Briglen soldiers? Could they hear? Could the people inside the ball hear? What were the limits of a siren song?

Wisteria didn't know, but she would break them.

I need a song of peace. I need to stop this senseless war. To end the violence in men's hearts.

After all, women always finish the wars men start.

She would sing until her voice deserted her, sing until the armies threw down their weapons and went home. She would sing until Ari's eyes opened and met hers once more.

Or, more realistically, she would sing until her song killed her.

The tingling feeling from before returned and sank into her soul. The consequences of her song were hungry, and they wriggled inside her like eels, voraciously scrounging for something they could devour.

As Wisteria watched, the injury on Ari's arm began to glow.

The onlookers gasped, and a handful swore. Someone put their hand on her shoulder, but someone else jerked them away.

Golden light shone from Ari's body. It stitched his skin back together, quelled the swelling on his face, and settled in his chest like a miniature sunbeam. Ari gasped and wheezed, his brown eyes fluttering open. "... Wish ... ?"

She only smiled. A few tears dripped off her cheeks onto his, but she couldn't reply.

"Wish . . ." He sounded hoarse. His eyes widened more, and he jerked upright. "I had it—I had the antidote—"

He'd lost it back in Lady Ambrosia's grotto, but she couldn't tell him that. Couldn't tell him it didn't matter anyway. She couldn't stop singing. Not until either the poison or her song silenced her soul. Ari's skin still glowed, and she didn't want to stop—not until she knew he would live, even if she didn't.

"Your Highness, please, let us—" A spectator reached for the prince.

"Stay back!" Ari held out a hand, but his eyes were fixed on Wisteria. "Wish—what are you doing? Did you find a song?"

She shook her head, and a few tears trickled down her cheeks. Her friend was *alive*.

She winced as the song burrowed into her body with exploding pinpricks of pain that felt like a pufferfish being driven into every nerve.

"You . . . you *wrote* one? But—but you don't know how to do that safely! You could *die*!" Ari reached up and cupped her cheeks.

"Wish—Wish, please stop this. You have a chance to live. I have the antidote. If you drink it, you can be free. Lady Ambrosia can't . . ." He glanced down at the steps. "Wish . . . where's the antidote? I had it—I had it in the grotto. We were so close." His voice broke. "Stop. Please. I can't let you die for me. This isn't *fair*."

Murmurs rippled through the crowd. Some even began to hum along, bolstering Wisteria's spirits. Her song grew even louder as it reached the climax. She tried to shove it farther than the castle grounds, prayed a seabreeze would carry it to the armies. And, though she couldn't be sure if it was a vision or a figment of her own imagination, she could almost see the soldiers as they marched between thickets of trees. They halted, turning their faces to the sky.

"Do you hear that?" they whispered to each other. "That song . . ."

Wisteria's voice was fading, but she couldn't let her song die just yet. She imagined herself there amidst the invaders like a songbird on the branches. She would stop their march. She would fill them with love, with understanding. With peace.

"Why are we fighting?" the soldiers murmured amongst themselves.

"Why are we here?"

"Why do we need this blasted war?"

She smiled and closed her eyes, thinking of Ambrosia's girls. Now under the waves, Wisteria turned her attention to the grotto, where the fifteen other poor enslaved girls huddled in fear. Wisteria poured her song out for them, to calm their worries, to give them peace and comfort.

They could be free, too. They could sing her song.

Join me, Wisteria begged in her thoughts, and somehow her music conveyed those sentiments. *Please. Keep Iylamor safe and peaceful, even after my death.*

"Wisteria?" a hesitant voice asked, and Wisteria heard it as if she were in the room with them. Someone else reached for the speaking girl and dragged her back. It was all right, though. Wisteria was used to being the outcast; she was used to having Lady Ambrosia drive a wedge between her and the other girls.

Don't be scared. I need your help. If you so choose, take up my song. Help me stop this senseless war that men started and Lady Ambrosia continued. We don't have to be scared of her. We can fight. I stabbed her. I made her bleed—maybe I even killed her. There are more powerful things than fear in this world, and she knows that. That's why she wanted to drive us apart, make us afraid of loving one another.

Because there is more strength in love than fear, and together, we can be free.

Gasps and whispers flew back and forth between the girls. Some shrank into the shadows, while others drifted closer to the grotto door.

If we work together, we can free everyone.

Only one girl—the very same girl who had called Wisteria's name—spoke. "How do we join you?"

Sing. Think about those you love most, and sing.

The once-captive mermaids glanced at each other. Slowly, the first girl opened her mouth. Her voice, pure and sweet, seemed to lighten the mood. She gestured for the girls around to draw near, but only one other joined her. Yet, as she took the first mermaid's hand, she also sang. One took the high harmony, her voice light and soprano, while the other took the low harmony, a husky alto. Together, they held strong, even when Wisteria's strength wavered.

The song almost seemed to solidify inside Wisteria's throat, forming a hard lump that cut off the notes and her oxygen. Her vision faded, and she curled into a ball at the bottom of the palace's twenty-nine steps. Somehow, it felt fitting to die on an oddly-numbered staircase. At least she hadn't been nineteen at her death. Twenty was such a nice, even number . . .

"Wish!" That was Ari's voice. She could recognize it. Arms held her—were they his?

If they were, he pulled her close to his chest. "Wish—you're bleeding. It's all right. I'm here. I've got you. Stay with me . . ."

Did we do it? She tried to ask, but her voice refused to cooperate. Speaking felt like jamming a rock against another rock and expecting one to crumble.

Something wet dripped onto her skin. Tears? Rain? Ocean mist? She didn't know.

Far off, she heard the other mermaids gathering, all of them singing her song.

They could stop Lady Ambrosia's war. They could reinstate the peace between Iylamor and Briglen.

"You saved my life," Ari whispered.

Wisteria smiled. She had.

What a good choice.

~∾∾~

Wisteria heard the singing first.

It swaddled her in an airy, weightless breeze that washed all the pain from her body. The music felt like the tide bringing her to shore, sweeping her away from the depths of the ocean and onto the sand.

Then there was weight on her, around her, *in* her. Gravity engulfed her, as did something else: a pair of arms.

She could feel their strength, their warmth, even as a chill sank into her bare arms and legs. Her eyes fluttered open, and she blinked as dim firelight illuminated Ari's face hovering over her own.

"Wish!" He clutched her to his chest and buried his face in her hair. "You're alive. You did it."

Wisteria opened her mouth to ask a flurry of questions, but talking *still* felt like a rock beating against another rock. So she closed her mouth and focused on her surroundings.

She sat on a pink-quilted bed with matching pink draperies encircling her. The gauzy pink barrier partially obscured her view of the bedroom beyond, but she could make out seashell-themed decor and a large bay window. In the corner, a grandfather clock ticked away, reminding her that she didn't know how much time had passed since she'd lost consciousness. Moonlight filtered through the window, one of the few clues that a handful of hours had passed. That, and the fact that someone had taken her out of her dress and put her in a frilly, white, short-sleeved nightgown.

She shifted her gaze to Ari. Whole. Uninjured. *Alive.*

She opened her mouth. *What happened?*

Nothing came out.

Several more tries were equally unfruitful, so she jostled Ari until he released her and she could straighten to a sitting position. She speared him with a questioning look.

The prince raised his hands, surrendering to her curiosity. "Briglen arrived with a treaty around noon today. My advisors are poring over it in the library, but I think . . . I think it will usher in a new era of peace." He tucked a strand of hair behind her ear. "So I regret to inform you that it looks like we will not be tomb-mates anytime soon."

Wisteria's shoulders shook as she laughed, but her amusement produced no noise besides the air leaving her nose. The lack of sound quickly sobered her, and she reached up to touch her throat. *Ari?* She made a few more gestures to help him understand. *Ari, why can't I talk?*

He let out a puff of air, and his brows furrowed together. "Can . . . can you not say anything?"

She shook her head and tapped her throat again.

"You used a powerful song to stop the army. More powerful than any siren before, I'd wager." He tried to smile, but the tears on his cheeks contradicted some of his cheerfulness. "Maybe this is just a side effect. I'm sure your voice will return if we give it time."

Or this is what the song stole from me. Wisteria's mind flickered back to what she'd prayed right before she started singing—how she'd offered her voice and even her tail if she could stop the war.

And, as their long searches in the library had discovered, every song had a cost.

Oh, no! Wisteria threw off the covers. She pulled the fabric of her nightgown up as much as she dared and felt the bare skin there.

Not a single black-and-gold scale decorated her pale skin.

She tottered on the edge of hyperventilating. Her scales, her precious scales, the proof of her mermaid nature . . . *gone*.

Ari uttered a strangled moan. When Wisteria twisted around to face him, a blush darkened his cheeks. "I was worried about that."

Why? What happened? Wisteria grasped his shoulder, and he continued without much prodding.

"After Briglen arrived, a handful of other mermaids who had been enslaved by Lady Ambrosia came ashore. They said you told them to keep guard over Iylamor, to keep the peace." Ari cleared his throat, and, though he didn't look, he tugged the covers up over her legs again. "They found the antidote back in the grotto and brought it for you." He stared at the bedcovers, and this time, Wisteria guessed it wasn't for the sake of propriety. "But when I got you to swallow the antidote, your tail didn't come back like it should have." His hand found hers. "I thought about Scylla and everything we learned, and—well, songs change people. So I got to worrying that . . . maybe the song stole your mermaid tail as punishment. Which means . . . I don't know if you'll be able to go back to the sea. Not . . ." His thumb was cold as it brushed across her knuckles. "Not to live there, anyways."

A wave of sorrow crashed over Wisteria. True, she'd been captive underwater for the last ten years, but the ocean was the only life she'd ever known. She'd been born there. Played hide-and-seek with Prim in the coral. Buried both parents in the seabed.

As much as it'd been a prison, the ocean was her home.

She clutched the sheets in a fist. Silent sobs wracked her shoulders as more memories flooded her mind. Memories of her father, with his deep, steady voice, taking her on trips to learn about marine life. Her mother, who would tuck Wisteria into her seaweed bed at night and tell her fairy tales. Things that Wisteria hadn't allowed herself to think about in the last decade crashed through her, their tenderness a sorrow she couldn't bear. And now, free of the Sea Witch, she couldn't even go back to her old home, to the beautiful life she'd known before the tragedy.

Her voice, her tail, her life. She'd offered all three to the song, and it had taken them all, though in different ways.

Ari's grip tightened on her hand. The world teetered and held its breath for a moment, but Wisteria didn't understand *why* until Ari blurted out, "Wish—I'm sorry. It's all my fault. I cost you everything."

He pulled her close to him. Their arms and sorrows tangled up together, intertwined as deeply as their lives and fates had always been.

"Stay here," Ari murmured against her temple. "You saved my kingdom and my life. It's the least I can do."

Wisteria would have refused the nicety on the grounds of it being offered out of obligation until Ari added, "Please."

She pulled back to look at him. His gaze held hers, his dark eyes pleading. "I want you to stay. It's selfish of me, I know." Ari's fingers brushed across her cheek, and she sucked in a breath as something like a jellyfish sting—but more pleasant—raced through her. "I won't keep you here against your will, but I need you to know that I want you here with me. Do *you* want to stay?"

Stay?

Wisteria swallowed. A choice. He'd offered her a choice. To stay, to make a new home and a new life, to start a new adventure. Not one forced upon her, but one she could willingly pursue if it interested her.

He'd given her a chance to have her own voice.

Wisteria nodded, smiling despite the tears.

Yes.

LA LLORONA

The story of La Llorona is shared around every fireside in México. Parents warn disobedient children to behave, lest they be snatched away by the infamous Weeping Woman. Boys and girls boast about close encounters, moments when they've only narrowly avoided La Llorona's skeletal grasp.

But if they knew the truth, perhaps they would not be so quick to use her name as nothing more than legend.

Because a demon like La Llorona is not one to be fought unawares.

Hands wrapped around my neck.
Cold water stole my breath.
Black.
Blue.

Water dripped from my tattered white dress as I stood on the edge of my tiny village. Mud squelched under my feet with every step I took. I shuffled toward the cobblestone path, which was half-eaten with sand and dead sprouts of grass.

I clutched my little sister's cold hand. Eliana squeezed my bony fingers with her own trembling ones, and I returned the gesture.

The river we'd climbed out of churned mere meters behind us. Something hissed beneath those waves. If I had looked back, I might have seen the flash of a blue-and-green fin or even a hand waving me away on my quest.

In the distance, a woman wailed. "My *children*! My *children*!"

"Mami sounds upset, Xiomara," Eliana whispered. "Please stay here with me. We can just go back into the river and forget everything that happened. We can look at all the stars and make hundreds of wishes."

I gritted my teeth and tried to keep my angry words, as sharp and biting as piranhas, inside. "I have to do this, Eliana. We'll stargaze later." Even if I barely understood this new, burgeoning magic within me, I couldn't let tonight pass from my grasp. I had to trust myself—and the instincts that had been brought to life with my death and rebirth as a creature of the water.

I screamed, bubbles exploding from my mouth.

No one heard.

No one.

"This isn't right," Eliana mumbled.

I whipped around, my grip tightening on her hand. She flinched and ducked her head. I swore at myself; I hadn't intended to spook her. *I* wasn't the monster here.

Moving more slowly, I drew her into an embrace. "I'm not going to hit you, love. I would never hurt you."

Eliana bobbed her head and sniffled. Gently, I combed my fingers through her damp hair and kissed her cheeks. She needed to know I was different from those who had hurt her before, different from the evil spirits who had haunted our house. Even now, the ghosts of their actions lingered on my skin. Old bruises throbbed on my neck, as painful as when they'd first been delivered—back when I was human.

"You heard what Abuela told everyone in town. The *velorio* is today." The *velorio*—our funeral wake. I caressed Eliana's cheeks, the blue scales that decorated her copper-colored skin rough beneath my fingertips. "It wouldn't be very polite for a corpse to keep her own guests waiting, would it?" I asked with a wry twist to my lips.

"But . . . if Papi did come visit . . . and Papi and Mami are both there . . ." Eliana lifted her hands to finally return my hug. Her fingers dug into my spine, and her whole body trembled.

"Papi isn't coming back. And even if he's there, Mami will be so overjoyed to see him, they won't fight with each other." I gave her a final kiss and pulled away. "Go back into the water with Aracely. It's warm there, and I won't be gone too long."

"Xiomara . . ."

"I won't die a second time. I promise." I stepped onto the cobblestone path before she could make me promise *no one* would die tonight.

My bare feet made no sound against the stone as I wound into the heart of the village. My heartbeat reverberated in my ears, and the *plop* of the river water that dripped off me was the rhythm of a war drum. I wove my way between the wood and clay houses, a one-woman march to battle.

Plop. Plop. Plop.

I shivered and rubbed my arms, which were marked with scales and goosebumps underneath my thin nightgown. If I'd known I'd die on that fateful night, I would have dressed more appropriately for the afterlife.

"Xiomara, *please* come back. *Please.* I just want to watch the stars together." Despite Eliana's pleas, despite how my heart ached at her sweet request, I refused to slow down. I couldn't go back, but I didn't want her to come with me, either. She'd be safer in the river, away from the *velorio* and the chilly autumn air.

My head cracked against a rock in the riverbed. Blood turned the water crimson. My limbs lost all resistance, my vision darkening. I sank lower and lower as our attacker plunged my sister into the icy depths.

Eliana thrashed. Clawed at her attacker. Every fiber in my being wanted to reach out and help her, but I couldn't. My arms were too weak, too sluggish. I would never be able to save my sister.

Memories flashed through me, whipping the piranhas inside me into a frenzy. *Unfair. Not right.* My breath quickened; my fists clenched. I knew, I *knew*, it might be best to let unfinished business rest in peace. To take the second chance at life the sirens had given us and forget our previous one, just like Eliana wanted.

But every time I thought I should give up the ghost of my revenge, my piranhas protested and my thoughts turned back to the simple phrase: it wasn't fair. How could we forget that our murderer still haunted our old village? How could I allow them to live while my precious sister had died?

Branches rattled against each other. A biting gale ripped a few remaining leaves free—crinkled, crackling orange flags that were carried away on the wind. Lost, separated. Dead.

I felt a strange sort of kinship with those doomed leaves.

Stars glittered in the sky, bright and beautiful. They led me to the center of town, pointing me to my destination. Most of the houses in our quiet village were shuttered up, save for ours. Light spilled from it onto the street, painting the night with warmth and bright color.

Even from a few doors down, I could see the people crammed into our one-story house. A few of the rowdy neighborhood boys leaned over the windowsills, trying to crawl inside the house. The light, the atmosphere, the laughter, the *people* held some strange, ordinary magic. Perhaps some people called it love. Whatever it was, it decorated the street and brought nearby concrete houses to life.

I scowled as I watched the neighbor boys' antics. I shouldn't have expected them to be sad at my *velorio*—they had often pulled, pinched, and bullied me—but the least they could do was be silent and show some decency. After all, it had only been two weeks since my death. Instead, two of them poked at each other while a third grabbed tamales and retreated back outside. They glanced my way, but I sank back into the shadows of a neighbor's house where the light couldn't expose me.

The wind gusted, and one of the youths shuddered. "Feels like a ghost."

The third one wiggled his tamale at the others. "Maybe it's Xiomara or Eliana come back from the dead. Careful—they may snatch you!" As the tamale-wielding boy spoke, he leapt toward his friend.

Tía Julieta stuck her curly head out the window to shush the boys. I'd been on the receiving end of her rants far too many times and had no desire to stick around for another. Even an eternal afterlife was too short to waste time on that.

I drifted toward the sound of a woman's wailing.

Mami.

"My children!" she keened. Her cry carried across the night like the wind's howl. Nearby trees rattled like skulls, and I could not blame them. Mami must have terrified them, too.

I scanned my house, searching for her. Each room in my old house possessed a window. Mami's room and the living room were closest to me, their windows thrown open. In the living room, someone had set up a candlelit table filled with food. More of my neighbors, uncles, aunts, and cousins crowded around there. But I located Mami in her bedroom, clothed in gray with a red shawl wrapped around her shoulders, her hair pulled up in elaborate braids that crisscrossed her head. Abuela stood next to her chair, arms crossed, a stern scowl etched onto her face.

Behind her, more candles burned on a table that was packed with presents and a black-and-white family photo taken a few years ago. In the picture, frozen forever in time, all four of us stared at the camera: Papi, Mami, Eliana, and myself.

"First my husband leaves me, and now the river takes my children," Mami sobbed to my grandmother. She dabbed at her eyes with the embroidered handkerchief I'd made for her birthday. "Even my precious baby, my sweet Eliana. She was so young—so beautiful!"

I crept closer. The piranhas inside me grew even more violent and impatient as my desperation to see justice served multiplied. To end the unrelenting repetition in my head of *it isn't fair, it isn't fair, it isn't fair, it isn't fair.*

Abuela patted Mami's shoulder, and Mami sniffled loudly. Her bedroom seemed to be designated for mourning, while in the common area, people laughed as they celebrated two lives that had been short but, for the most part, loved.

Outlined by the living room door, portly Tío Tadeo held a glass of wine in one hand and gesticulated animatedly with his other. Always the center of attention, that one, recognizable by his signature mustache and hearty laugh. His booming voice spread the magic and intimacy of the *velorio* wherever it could be heard. ". . . and, of course, Xiomara chased the dog throughout the whole city to get her shoe back." Tío Tadeo shook his fist and pitched his voice higher to imitate five-year-old me. "'*You come back here, you filthy stealing mutt!*'" He chuckled and sipped his drink. "Xiomara was always such a stubborn girl."

Plop, plop, plop went the water as it dripped off the hem of my white nightgown. Inside my chest, the piranhas snapped and writhed, putting every nerve in my body on edge. They would not be satiated until I acted, until justice was served.

The siren Aracely had given me a few lessons about using my newfound power, but for the most part, instinct and magic fueled me. With intuition as my guide, I clung to the shadows and opened my mouth.

Helpless. I was so helpless. Impotent rage and betrayal bubbled up into a scream that the water carried away, heard by no human ear.

But something else lurked in the waters, and it heard.

I poured all those emotions—the betrayal, the rage over my sister's shed blood—into my siren song. My arm itched and burned as new, fresh scales began sprouting near my elbow. If I kept singing, I might lose the small vestiges of humanity I had left. Still, I sang.

A creature of the depths, scaly and almost reptilian, glided closer with a few flicks of her tail. "You poor soul," the siren whispered.

Somehow, I understood the strange, chattering language. Webbed claws stretched toward me, and I didn't shudder. I wanted to grasp them, to cling to one last chance of life. The piranhas inside of me twisted my stomach, stoked by my desperation to reach out and take my heart's desire.

Help me, I screamed with my soul. Help me, please!

The scales crept closer to my wrist.

Mami glanced up. "Do . . . do you hear that?" She stood, drifting away from Abuela to the bedroom window. "Do you hear singing?"

"Leandra, sit down." Abuela moved closer. "I don't hear anything. You're imagining things."

Mami tightened her shawl around her shoulders. "Maybe . . ."

I focused on my memories of Papi. He'd been tall, strong, with a thick mustache and a tiny curl that always fell onto his forehead. A handful of memories rushed in, deepening the pull of my magic. Memories of him taking Eliana and me to the riverside to swim on hot days. Of long nights where he dutifully taught us all the names of the constellations and how to find the North Star using *la Osa Mayor*. Of him positioning my fingers on his guitar's strings so I might coax some beautiful melody out of the instrument.

My song fed off these emotions and recollections. The shadows twisted to form his tall, lean build—a trick of the eye, but powerful to one enthralled by my magic. The melody crescendoed, and the illusion turned it into what Mami desired to hear most: my father's music.

Mami gasped. "Reyes?"

"Leandra." Abuela strode over to Mami and grasped her shoulders. "It isn't Reyes." She muttered a long list of insults directed at my father and his philandering ways. Things like, *what man would forsake his wife, abandon his family, and fail to mourn his children?*

I pushed memories of Papi playing guitar to the forefront of my mind. The sorrow, the grief, the terror I'd felt whenever Mami and Papi fought. When she'd hit him, lash out. And the anger and abandonment I'd felt on the day he'd left—without taking Eliana and me.

All of these were my papi. The good. The bad. The wrong. The right.

But I would not abandon my family as he had. I would not think only of self-preservation, but also of justice. Not for myself, but the one truly innocent member of our family. Eliana.

Her death would not go unavenged.

The burning in my arm deepened as my song swelled with power.

"Madre, let go!" Mami shook Abuela off. "How can you not see it? It's Reyes! I knew he'd come back—I just *knew* he'd come back when he heard about our girls!"

"Leandra! Stop this nonsense!" Abuela commanded. "The grief has made you delirious."

She reached for Mami, but Mami slapped her hand away.

"Don't treat me like a child, Madre!" Mami snapped. "I can hear Reyes singing."

"Reyes is with his mistress." Abuela crossed her arms. Where Mami was a raging fire of fury, Abuela was a cold, freezing sort of wrath. "When will you realize he's not coming back?"

"He is!" Mami shrieked. "I wrote to him when the girls died. He *will* come back to me!"

"You wrote him? *Mija*—what good can come of contacting that pig?" Abuela grabbed Mami's shoulders. But my mother whirled around and struck Abuela across the face.

The smack resonated in the night.

"Don't touch me!" Mami yelled.

Abuela's shoulders straightened. She pulled herself up to her full height like she meant to intimidate Mami. Abuela already stood a head taller, but in her shadow, in the force of Mami's disobedience, Abuela seemed to grow even more. "How dare you," Abuela said, her voice controlled, but icy and barbed. "Don't disrespect me."

"*You* don't tell me how to deal with *my family*. They are *mine*!" Mami snarled.

The *velorio's* magic cracked slightly, just enough to reveal the filth underneath the familial charade, the dark side of what love lived here.

And I came from the filth. I came from the madness, and maybe it burned in me, too. I would only use it for good, though. For justice. To protect Eliana. The thought of my sister—her precious face, how I would keep it from ever being bruised again—strengthened my magic, too. I would not be my mami. This madness would end with me.

Mami scrambled over the windowsill. Nothing could stop Mami's mania where Papi was concerned.

Especially with my siren song strengthening the spark of obsession that resided inside her blood, driving her to insanity.

"Reyes?" Mami called.

"Leandra! Come back here." Abuela leaned out the window, but our sensible, strict grandmother would never replicate Mami's dramatics. Nor did my song affect her, for Abuela was not my victim on this cold night. "Reyes is gone and your children are dead, *mija.*"

Rage burned in my chest, hot enough to keep the chill out of my river-soaked bones. I darted back into an alley, Mami giving chase, lured on by a song only she could hear.

Mami reeled around the corner after me. If Abuela continued calling to Mami, the sound didn't carry to me. Invisible to others' eyes, I scurried down a different alley, weaving between colorful, decorated houses. I was a haunting, a punishment, just for my beloved Mami.

"Reyes!" Mami followed, always a little bit behind. "Reyes, stop, please!"

In less than a minute, we reached the riverbank. Mami skidded to a stop and glanced around. "Reyes, *please*. I need you. I don't know how to live without you and our girls." Groaning, she dropped to her knees. "I don't care about your mistress. Please. Come back." She picked up a rock and tossed it into the water; ripples shattered the reflection of the stars and the moon. "Our children . . ." She dared to reach toward the water like she might try and caress it as one would a loved one's face. "They're dead. Fierce Xiomara . . . sweet Eliana . . ."

Fierce Xiomara. Sweet Eliana.

The piranhas could take no more. They swarmed inside my chest, stirred up by thoughts of *how dare she! Unfair! Not right!*

"Tell the truth, Leandra." I revealed myself in the moonlight, in all my siren glory, clothed in nothing but a wet nightgown with my bare feet against the riverbank. Scales crept up my neck and face; I could feel that itching burn deepening as they formed, their appearance the price of unleashing my magic. My damp, twisted hair dangled past my waist. "Your daughters didn't just die. You *killed* them. And then you ran back to the village, claiming to be the victim, as the poor martyr who lost everything." I trembled as I stood before my mother, her sins laid out on the riverbank behind us.

My mother murdered me. The thought screamed through my mind, through my struggling being as my life ebbed away. But as I tottered on the brink of death—or perhaps right when I had crossed over—I heard, for the first time, a siren's enthralling voice, calling me back from beyond.

"I can help you, my innocent one," Aracely whispered, her webbed fingers caressing my face, her tone softer than my mother's had ever been. "I can make you one of us."

When the magic had done its work, had taken my breath and given it back, I was a siren. Something to be feared. And a new thought tickled my mind, as fresh and sharp as the magic that now lived within me.

My mother had murdered me. But now she would pay. I could make her pay for ending my life, for ending Eliana's life.

My dear, darling Mami.

"Xiomara?" Mami whispered. "*Mija*?" Her face twisted, and she clutched at the rosary around her neck.

"How ironic, you using that word." I snorted. *My daughter. My dear. My darling.* "Because you always hated me. But Eliana? She was your favorite. She adored you."

Eliana peeked out of the water.

"Get *down*." My voice carried a steely edge.

"No." Eliana's eyes darted between the two of us. "Mami, please. I'm sorry about Papi. I'm sorry if I did something bad. I love you."

"Oh, Eliana." Mami rose and stumbled forward, arms outstretched.

I stepped between them. "No. Don't apologize, Eliana. You did nothing wrong. Don't come any closer, Mami. You will *never* touch my sister again."

Mami shook her head. "No, no—you don't understand. I never wanted to hurt you. I—your father. He did this."

"Papi didn't kill us." I glanced at the river behind me; bubbles drifted up to the surface and the flash of a tail caught my eye. "You did."

I trod backward into the river's embrace; the current snagged my nightgown. Funny—the water had been so cold when Mami tried to drown me. But now its warmth filled me with power.

Deeper and deeper I moved until the water reached my chest. Eliana clutched the back of my nightgown. She tugged me closer to her, trembling all the while. Her tail flicked back and forth and brushed my legs several times; I could feel the struggle in her arms as she tried to stay immobile and attached to me instead of letting the river sweep her downstream.

"Come in, Mami," I called in a sing-song voice. "Come into the water. Don't you want to see what it's like to drown?"

My magic settled into Mami's soul once more and she drifted forward, her eyes glassy. Perhaps if she hadn't been ensnared by my song, she might have spotted the small feminine face that peered out of the water and smiled with a mouth full of fangs. Perhaps Mami might have recognized the flip of a tail that passed right by her.

Scales crept down my legs and stitched them together. How painful the transformation had been the first time—and how natural it felt this time. The metaphorical magic of the *velorio* had seemed light, cheery, and familiar. A beacon of my life before the drowning. But even magic hadn't been able to cover up the abuse, the bruises, the screaming and fighting. A pretty veneer, but thin and conditional.

The magic of the river, however—the *real* magic—felt intoxicating. Those who hadn't embraced the magic might fear it as dark, chaotic, dangerous. But that ugly misconception also couldn't hide the vicious love that burst from the depths and guided me to my future.

I flicked my beautiful blue fluke, one just like my sister's and Aracely's, and smiled.

"I'm *scared*, Xio," Eliana whispered. Her grip tightened the fabric against my skin and tethered her to me.

I know, I wanted to say, but I couldn't stop singing lest the trance over Mami end. *I'm going to make sure you're never scared again.* Never again would I have to cover my sister's ears as we listened to Mami scream in the next room. Never again would I have to pick shards of clay out of our heels while Eliana justified that our mother hadn't *meant* to throw a plate at us—it had slipped. Never again would I allow Eliana to make excuses for a woman who could, depending on her volatile mood, cover my sister in kisses or bruises.

No matter what I had to do, I would keep Eliana safe, even if I lost part of my soul to do it.

Bolstered by the thoughts of Eliana, my ethereal melody soared into the night air. Mami waded closer until the water reached her waist. The currents tugged at her skirts, and her arms moved to keep her afloat and on course. I doubted she could reach the bottom now. With a final high note, I cut off my song, ceasing the enchantment. For better or for worse, I wanted Mami to be herself in this climactic moment. To be fully aware of her punishment, if not her wrongdoings.

Mami blinked a few times as if she'd awakened from a dream. "Wait—no. *No.*" She whipped her head around before her gaze alighted on me. Her chest heaved, and I allowed myself a moment to revel in her widening eyes and slack jaw. "Impossible! You're . . . you're supposed to be *dead*," she whispered.

"But, despite your best efforts, we live. Though . . ." I guided Eliana out of hiding and ran one wet hand down the scales on her cheek. She shuddered, tears spilling over her eyelashes. "Needless to say, we've changed quite a bit."

"Are you evil spirits—*demons*?" Mami tried to swim away, but Aracely's fin flicked her in the back. She yelped and covered her face with her hands, twisting around. "Am I in Hell?"

I bared my teeth. "Not *yet*. You killed us, but the sirens' magic floods this river, and they saw everything." Several slate-blue heads rose from the water surrounding Mami and I. Dark hair floated around them in the current like snakes. "Eliana and I were pure of heart. When we died, the sirens imbued us with their magic and made us one of their own."

"So you *are* a *hija del diablo*," Mami spat.

"Not nearly as much as you are."

Mami's eyes blazed as they locked on mine. "Don't you dare talk about your mother that way."

"I would never." I closed my eyes and let the water fill my senses. Swallow me whole. Its roar engulfed me; its power swelled up inside me like I had its currents running through my veins. Opening my eyes again, I gazed at her, my face half sneer, half snarl. "But the river gave birth to Eliana and I anew. You are no longer our mother."

"You can't replace me! I'm your *mami*!" She dove for me clumsily, hands outstretched. Instinct made me spread my arms to further shield Eliana—protecting her was my second nature by now. Eliana's scream echoed across the water, but Mami's blow never landed on either of us.

For the first time, someone else jumped in to protect *me*. Aracely leaped out of the water and raked her sharp claws across Mami's abdomen. Shrieking, Mami fell backward with a great splash. She plunged beneath the waves, and I thought the current might sweep her away. But before my hopes could rise too much, she resurfaced, sputtering and hacking.

Waves crashed against each other as the water rose, violent and angry, as it often did after a huge thunderstorm. The sirens rose with the waves, their expressions twisted. With bared teeth, they converged on Mami.

"I don't want to watch!" Eliana bawled. She grasped my arm. "Xiomara, make it end!"

I scoffed. "If her death is an injustice, then the river will right the wrong. She'll be reborn as a siren, just like we were. Just like all the sirens before us."

"Get away!" Mami smacked at the water. The sirens dodged her assault, and Aracely landed another strike. Mami might have screamed, but a fierce wave dragged her under the water. She somehow managed to fight the current and pop back up, cursing us and her attackers.

The anticipation of victory welled up inside of me and blinded me to everything else. Victory and justice . . . Soon, I would have them both—and no one would ever hurt me or my sister again.

"Xio!" Eliana tugged harder on my arm, jerking my attention away from my moment of triumph. "Stop it! Mami didn't mean to hurt us!"

"She *killed* us!" I screeched. All the injustice boiled over: the abuse, the attempted murder, the audacity Mami possessed to *mourn* the very thing she destroyed. It was just an act to gain sympathy and save her own reputation. "She beat us, dragged us from our beds, and drowned us. The sirens saw. The sirens *saved* us!"

"I don't *care*! You sound just like our parents. Like what they used to say—Papi did this, so he *deserves* that. Mami did that, so *she* deserves this." Eliana pounded me with her fist. "I'm so tired of fighting, Xio. Tell the sirens to let her go!"

For a brief moment, I forgot to fight the current, and it swept me under. Had I been carried away by my own madness, too? Had I become just like Mami? If I had, perhaps it was best to let the river take me. Wash me and my sins away so Eliana could be happy with the sirens. They would protect her. Perhaps I, too, was too tainted by my family's bloodline.

But the river did not take me—it could not fight against Eliana's hold. For all the times I had supported her, this time, with strength that belied her age, she pulled me back above the waves.

Her arms wrapped around my neck and pulled me close. "Let Mami go, Xiomara."

With sweet tenderness, my sister kissed my cheek. Suddenly, I didn't know whether the wetness there was from the river or my own tears. Here I was, on the cusp of fulfilling my deadly unfinished business, and yet . . . I couldn't do it.

Aracely and the sirens battered my mother. She swatted at them, howling obscenities and pleas. "I'm innocent!" Mami yelled. Her long skirts tangled in the undertow, and her wide eyes found my sister. "Tell them, girls. *I'm* the victim. Your father is the monster. He *abandoned* us. How was I supposed to support all of us?" Mami's eyes burned with the same histrionic fire that had consumed her the night she'd killed us.

I gathered Eliana in my arms and cradled her close to my chest. "Aracely, wait." At my command, the sirens paused their attack, though it might have been too late. Blood marred Mami's dress, her bare arms and cheeks scratched and bitten. A few sirens hissed their displeasure, but I ignored them. "Are you ready to make amends, Mami?"

"Yes, yes." Mami bobbed her head, stretching out her arms. "Of course. Your father destroyed us, Xiomara. It isn't right that we should still suffer."

I gritted my teeth. The piranhas in my chest snapped, enraged by her answer, but I tried to ignore them. I would not succumb to them again; I would not be like her. "Papi isn't the only one who destroyed us."

"Come here, Eliana. Come to your mami," Mami cooed. She beckoned my sister closer.

"Eliana . . ." Aracely warned. She glanced toward me, but I shook my head to tell her to wait. Around me, the river's currents also died down.

In the calmer waters, Eliana pushed herself out of my embrace and swam toward Mami. "I knew it was an accident, Mami. I knew it all along. You never meant to hurt us."

Mami cupped Eliana's cheek. "Of course, love. Of course. Come here."

"Mami, please. Say you're sorry." Eliana lifted her hands to our mother as if she wanted to be held.

I didn't move toward Mami, but I did sigh. My mother would never apologize—nor did I think she would change. But forgiveness lingered on the tip of my tongue, if only so I could free myself from the hatred and violence that permeated my family history.

Before I could loosen my tongue, though, *el diablo* loosened Hell instead.

Mami's hands flew to Eliana's neck, all pretense of a grieving mother gone. "Let me go!" Mami's face was twisted into a sneer, her eyes wide and red. "Let me go to the shore or I'll kill her again." She hoisted my sister out of the waves; Eliana clawed at Mami's ruthless fingers.

"*No!*" I lunged forward. "Mami, don't!"

My sister's tail thrashed in midair, her eyes wide as Mami tried to choke the life out of her a second time. I opened my mouth, ready to unleash my siren song and compel Mami to drop Eliana, but the first note never crossed my lips.

Aracely leapt out of the water and ravaged my mother's face.

Mami screamed, dropping Eliana. With a wild lunge, I snatched my sister and hugged her as the sirens swarmed Mami.

Eliana sobbed, and I had to hold back tears of my own. I quivered, my thudding heart deafening in my ears. I had come so close to losing my sister again. I'd let her get hurt once more.

"Shh. Shh." I ran my trembling fingers through her hair, murmured in her ear, tried to protect her from Mami's hysteric wails. My own stomach churned, but I could not afford to throw up, so I focused all my attention on my sister instead.

"Why?" Eliana shivered. She clutched my neck and buried her face against my shoulder.

I didn't know what she was asking, but I wouldn't have had the answers, anyway. I didn't know why Mami had chosen the way she had or what had driven her. I couldn't begin to fathom why she'd once more decided to attack when she could have protected and loved. So I could only hold her and try to block out the noises with whispers of "I love you."

The sirens' teeth ripped into Mami's skin; their talons tore at her clothes. Mami lashed at them with her shawl, but the limp, wet weapon could not repel a siren's fury. One of the sirens hissed and clamped her sharp teeth into Mami's side. The river pulled them under amidst Mami's wails.

Until the cries ceased.

The water turned crimson around me, but I didn't want to see the source. I sank down, down, down, until Eliana's arms wrapped around my neck in a tight embrace and her face pressed against my scales.

Aracely swam over to us. With her sunken slate-blue face, sharp teeth, gills, and serpentine eyes, she resembled something out of a child's nightmare, yet I felt no terror at her appearance.

"I am sorry for your loss," she whispered. Her claws grasped my shoulder. "But the river demands justice. She will not hurt you again."

I nodded, my throat thick with the forgiveness I'd never spoken into existence. The forgiveness Mami had never asked for, but that I offered even so.

I would not lose any more of my soul to hatred, bitterness, and fury like she had.

Aracely pressed a kiss against my cheek with lips stained by my mother's blood.

Eliana whimpered as Aracely raced away. I turned my attention to her. Always her. "Are you all right, love? Did she hurt you?"

Eliana shook her head. "Not too bad." Her voice faltered. "I guess . . . I guess you were right."

"No, Eliana. No, *you* were." I sniffed and rocked her in my arms, choking on my words. "I'm . . . I'm sorry. I'm sorry for everything. I don't want to be so angry, so much like Mami."

Eliana traced the scales on my cheek. "I know. And deep down . . . you're not like Mami. You're . . . you're a siren. A protector. Just like Aracely."

I seized her fingers and kissed them each in turn. The piranhas inside of me had dissipated. "I love you, Eliana. Thank you for reminding me about who I am today."

A sister. A protector. Someone freed from the bloody path my family had embraced for itself. Someone who could choose differently.

"You were right, though." Eliana rubbed her neck, her eyes downcast. "Mami hurt me. Again."

"We were both wrong and right in different ways. But don't think about it, love. It's all over. Mami can't hurt us anymore." I flicked my fins and propelled us closer to the surface. "Let's go look at the stars."

Eliana nuzzled closer to me as we crested. Above us, a full moon graced the sky with her bright light. The stars twinkled, a million diamonds scattered in a celestial sea.

A moan shattered the peace around us.

Eliana screamed my name. Wrapping my arms around her, I bared my teeth.

A skeletal hand thrust up from the water, latching onto the riverbank. The creature emerged—clothed in our mother's shredded, hole-dotted gray dress—and struggled to pull herself out of the water. Once she'd clawed her way onto the muddy shore, fog drifted from the river to roll around the hem of her dress.

Water puddled around the remains of her feet as she straightened and turned to face the river.

I covered Eliana's mouth before she could shriek again.

The creature no longer wore Mami's skin. A skull stared across the water—and fire burned in the empty eye sockets. I could feel them searching, *grasping* for me in the moonlight.

"*Querido Dios, protégenos,*" I whispered under my breath.

"*¡Ay, mis hijas!*" Mami wailed for her children just as she had in life, her voice shrill and cold. Even the trees quaked in terror when the autumn wind raced across their limbs, as if they wanted to uproot themselves and escape my mother.

I shivered, caught in Mami's frigid wrath as she called for us. I tightened my grip on Eliana. Her tears dripped onto my fingers, and I longed to swipe them away.

Mami—Mami's skeleton? Mami's ghost?—bent down and gathered up her shawl as it floated by her, half-sunk in the currents. She wrapped it around her shoulders, the tattered red like a smear of blood on a corpse.

"*¡Ay, mis hijas!*" she called again. Her jawbone clattered angrily. "*¡Mis hijas!*"

Mami wrapped her arms around herself and screamed, a sound so heartbreaking, so angry, that my shoulders tensed. Cold chills passed through my body. Shuddering, I dove under the water with Eliana and clenched my eyes shut.

Oh, how I wished the torment would pass. My body refused to relax, like it thought we were still back at home, captive and frightened. So many times, Mami had wailed like that to try and prevent Papi from leaving. Like she thought he'd stay if she could only act hysterical enough.

"Aracely!" I yelled. "Aracely, help!"

The screams slowly descended into a low moan.

I ground my teeth.

Waited.

A webbed hand pressed on my shoulder.

"She's back." I couldn't open my eyes. "Even *el diablo* could not contain my mother."

Aracely rubbed up and down my spine. "There is magic in the water, Xiomara. It transforms all that die here. But we did not accept her into our own, so she became a drowned spirit. Lost and condemned by her own anger."

"Will Mami be like that forever?" Eliana asked.

Aracely gnashed her fangs. "Until she atones for her sins. Until she feels true remorse."

I winced. The thought passed between the three of us, unspoken but heavy. Mami would truly be like this, a demon on earth, until the end of time.

Mami's voice drifted away from us. I resurfaced, Eliana still in my grasp. The fog Mami had raised thickened and consumed her form. Some kind of bittersweet emotion—sadness? relief? mourning?—sliced through me, as if I'd just watched one final piece of my mother be devoured. But the important part, her soul, had been consumed by her own selfishness years ago.

I swallowed. "I won't use it again."

Eliana lifted her wet face. "What?"

"The siren song. I won't use it again." Tears burned in my eyes. "I don't want to be that angry ever again."

"There is a time and place for anger," Aracely said. "The siren song is part of you now. Do not be afraid of it—learn when it is necessary to use it."

"I'll try and learn the difference." I stared at the empty spot where Mami had been, my mind spinning. I had a suspicion that, after tonight, it would take a long time to trust myself with my anger. But maybe one day, I might be able to understand Aracely's advice. "I promise."

Eliana sniffled and pressed a kiss to my nose. "I love you, Xiomara."

I rested our foreheads together. "I love you too, Eliana."

<div align="center">~~~</div>

Some people think that La Llorona drifts through the night looking for her lost children, but that simply isn't true. She knows where to find us.

No, she wails for revenge, recounting the night her sins caught up to her and stained the waters red.

So if you hear her shrieks carried on the wind late at night, lock your windows. For La Llorona seeks retaliation against children everywhere. But don't worry—if she tries to drown you in the river, you have nothing to fear.

For the sirens will hear your cries.

SALTWATER SOULS

Loneliness drove Dorothea to the shoreline.

It often did. She felt at home in the fog with a cardigan on, sitting with her toes half-buried in sand and waves. Moody, atmospheric, haunting . . . and the perfect place to cry. With the dunes and beach grass behind her, everything in the world seemed shut off. No honking cars, no bustling crowds, no nosy neighbors—which were all a staple in her small, northeastern oceanfront town. But here, *now*, Dorothea could have slipped between the pages of a vintage novel to become an Austen-esque protagonist and no one would have been the wiser.

The fog kissed her face and skin and lingered there in droplets, mingling with the tears already on her cheeks. She swiped the teardrops away, but they kept coming back, faster and faster, as if she might dissolve into nothing but saltwater.

She covered her face with her oversized sleeves and groaned.

I'm sorry for existing. I'm sorry I can't play by your rules. I'm sorry I take up space in the world and make you too uncomfortable.

Her soul screamed things when her lips wouldn't. And for the past hour, she'd been biting her tongue while her mother lectured her on the phone, saying everything Dorothea had heard before.

Just marry him! He's got money. He loves you. No—he adores you. What else do you need? You're too picky. You're too selfish. You're nothing but a heartbreaker, turning down anyone who likes you. You're going to die alone.

"But I don't love him like that!" Tears dampened Dorothea's lips as she wailed her innermost feelings to the frothing waves, who were her only confidant. "I *can't*." She hadn't loved *any* of the men who had pursued her—not in a romantic way. In all of her twenty-six years, she'd felt no connection that made her *want* to marry any of them. She'd tried to be their friend, tried to enjoy spending time with them, but eventually, the expectation came along that she would date them. And when she couldn't make the jump from platonic to romantic, her mother would always say the same thing, a sentiment which Dorothea echoed now to the ocean: "Maybe I'm too selfish to love *anyone*."

Romantic, platonic…maybe it didn't matter. Maybe what she called "love" was self-serving and shallow, no matter the term attached to it.

A large splash jerked her from her mourning.

Dorothea shoved herself upwards. The sand sucked her feet down, and she tripped once before she freed herself. Staggering forward, she raised her arm to shield her eyes, as if that might help her vision penetrate the thick fog.

Another splash. Someone gasped like a swimmer floundering in the deep.

Pure instinct propelled Dorothea into action. Her navy skirt, wet from the ocean, tangled around her gangly legs as she stumbled farther into the brine. No one else was around on this chilled morning to perform a rescue. Dorothea's heart pounded, almost louder than the crashing waves. "Hello? Is someone there? Are you okay?" She tottered and nearly lost her balance from the ebb and flow of the water. But with a few steps forward Dorothea found herself face to face with a woman who was half-buried in the ocean. Only her face and shoulders peeked out of the water—and that alone was enough for Dorothea to know this woman wasn't human.

The woman's hair rippled like the ocean itself as it fell in blue-gray waves. A tempest brewed inside her eyes, and three slits fluttered on either side of her neck. She wheezed like an asthmatic desperate for their inhaler, and, out of instinct, Dorothea reached to steady her. A webbed hand grasped Dorothea's forearm, fingers sharp like claws. But a glimpse of the woman's iridescent tail dispelled all doubts. Dorothea had found a mermaid.

Her mind revolted. How could this be? Mermaids were things of legend, of stories. Pretty pictures that Dorothea had often seen in books as a child. They were not real creatures she could touch. But even the best makeup artist in Hollywood couldn't replicate this woman's unique features.

Dorothea sucked in a breath. Should she be afraid? Even though her brain screamed yes, Dorothea couldn't muster any fear for herself, but only for this struggling woman—this struggling *mermaid*. "Can . . . can I help? Is something wrong?"

The woman brought her other arm out of the water. She cradled a speckled, pastel-colored egg as big as Dorothea's head in the crook of her arm.

"The egg—it's—it's hatching," the woman choked. Every syllable sounded forced, and she ducked her head back under the waves. When she resurfaced, she continued, "The baby will die if the egg hatches underwater. Our kind cannot breathe underwater until our gills come in."

"I—I don't understand. What do you mean?"

The woman sank beneath the water again. When Dorothea pulled her up, the poor woman gasped. "Mermaids must live on land, under the care of humans, from the time we hatch until we are eighteen."

Dorothea glanced behind her, but no one had invaded her private sliver of beach. Why would they, on such a melancholy day? She'd appreciated the solitude a few minutes ago, but now, she needed *help*. Her voice cracked and shook as she turned back to address the mermaid.

"I'm—I'm sorry. There's no one here besides me. I don't . . . do I need to give the egg to someone?"

The mermaid groaned. Her voice sounded hoarse until she dove back under and resurfaced. "The parents usually observe humans and select their favorite families to raise their children in loving homes. But I—this little one was not supposed to hatch until next year." The mermaid turned baleful eyes to her treasure. "But the egg—there was an accident right before our migration, and cracks have already formed. There is no time; my pod cannot tarry. Can you . . .?"

Dorothea's eyes widened as she met the woman's frantic gaze. "You mean, you want *me* to take the egg? Raise a *baby*?"

The woman coughed. Once more she had to wet her neck and face before she could speak. "Yes—*please*. If you do not want to raise the child until they return to the sea, there is a land pod that takes care of many mers. But the pod has already migrated to avoid the cold." She let a wave crest over her. Dorothea staggered from the force of the water, which soaked her from the shoulders down, and only barely managed to keep hold of the mermaid.

"Please, help me. At least keep the baby until the pod returns on the first of May."

Dorothea reached for the egg. Her fingers brushed against its wet, slimy surface, but she didn't draw back, even as the waves collided with her. How could she possibly care for a child? Children needed love, someone to take care of them. Dorothea was too selfish for the first and too incompetent for the second. If she couldn't love a man who would give her everything, how could she expect to love a baby who would *take* everything from her?

"*Please*," the mermaid begged. "The infant will hatch within days. Caring for them will be no different than caring for a human baby, I think." The mermaid's eyes reddened, and a tear slipped down her glittering cheek. "Do not let this child die."

Dorothea's heart cracked. Her bottom lip trembled, and she hated that she couldn't slap away the tears that trekked down her face. She couldn't do this. She couldn't take care of an infant, let alone a baby *mermaid* thrust upon her.

But she couldn't let this newborn die, either.

Dorothea adjusted her grip so she could cradle the egg with one arm and still support the mermaid with the other. "I won't let anything happen to the baby. I promise."

"Thank you." The mermaid squeezed Dorothea's arm. "Keep the child safe."

With that final plea, the mermaid pressed a kiss against the egg and let go of Dorothea. The woman gave one more teary wave before she swam toward the horizon, her tail the last thing visible before it, too, disappeared.

And Dorothea hugged the egg close to her chest, saltwater dripping from her eyes onto the sea's strange gift.

～〰〰～

"Dorothea Jo, you are *far* too selfish and unprepared for motherhood."

Dorothea held the wired teal phone against her ear, eyes staring listlessly at the ceiling. She lay in bed across a plush, robin-blue quilt. Why had she even called her mother in the first place? Ah, yes—because on the threshold of a life-changing event, she had wanted some advice, some comfort, someone to share the experience with.

She should not have called her mother for any of those, despite the yearning in her heart that told her this time, *this time*, surely things would be different. This time, her mother would *listen* to the million problems swirling around Dorothea's mind instead of add to them; this time, she wouldn't harp on things Dorothea had already vaguely considered and fretted over. Even a simple *"I believe in you"* would help Dorothea to face this terrifying new change that lurked in front of her . . . or, perhaps better yet, an offer of, *"I'll help you. I can watch the baby while you're at work."*

But no. Just like always, her mother's words cut her to the core and left her immobile and numb. Dim light filtered in from the muntin window on her right, casting a dreary filter on the room. She felt like a soldier in a fantasy novel, stabbed and left for dead, bleeding out on the battlefield as the world around her faded to gray.

Like a heroine on the verge of death stretching out for her beloved's face, Dorothea reached for the egg, which rested on a pillow beside her. She'd dried it upon re-entering her little stone cottage, though part of her wondered if she should have. But the mermaid had insisted the little one inside would die if the egg hatched underwater, so Dorothea assumed it didn't need to stay wet to hatch.

Such stress already, and she'd only been caring for this unborn soul for thirty minutes.

"Dorothea, are you there?"

Dorothea stretched out her feet, wriggling her toasty toes that were all snug in her woolen socks. "I'm here, Mom."

"Did you hear me? What makes *you* think you're fit for motherhood?" The voice on the line wasn't shrill, but it wasn't *comforting*, either. Rather, Dorothea's mother sounded the way she usually did: some strange mixture of demanding, accusing, and concerned.

"I don't . . ." Dorothea began but let her voice trail off until she could only hear the rain that pattered against her window. Her finger traced the outline of a shadow on her bed. The entirety of her small room seemed to be criss-crossed in x-shaped shadows, almost like a prison. "I don't know. I didn't really *pick* it, to be fair. I told you. I found an abandoned baby on the beach. I couldn't just leave it there." Her story sounded just as unbelievable the second time around, but more believable than *a mermaid gave me her egg.*

A huff. "Well, have you even thought about this whole ordeal? Are you even capable of giving a baby love, or will you get tired of it, too? Do you know how *expensive* children are? Do you think you have enough money to support a child? You work at a *library*, Dorothea."

Money. Dorothea hated the word. If not for money, she'd gallivant around the world. Get lost in other countries, embrace every culture, savor every experience life had to offer.

She swiped at the tears on her eyelashes. And now she'd have to worry about *two* mouths to feed when some days she could barely remember to feed her own. "I don't know."

"How very thorough." Dorothea's mother sighed. "And children need father figures, Dorothea. You are doing that baby a disservice if you raise it as a single woman. Children deserve stable, two-parent households. How do you think you'll provide that?"

"I . . ." Dorothea's mind felt bogged down with worries and arguments and her own heavy emotions. Her poor, overworked brain struggled to formulate an answer, but before she could even find her next syllable, her mother barged on, the answer already served on a silver platter.

"You could always marry Edward." Dorothea's mother didn't even have the decency to be hesitant as she broached the topic they'd quibbled about on their phone call that very morning. "He's rich. He adores you. And if you're so determined to be a mother, he could provide everything for this baby." A pause. "Do you even know all the legality that goes into this? Have you contacted a lawyer? Started the adoption process? There will be some hefty fees. I'm sure he could help."

"I don't know." Dorothea sucked in a ragged breath. Her cheeks felt stiff with dried tears, but more kept coming the longer she stayed on the phone. "I don't know anything, Mom. I've got to go, okay?"

"Dorothea—"

"No, I've really got to go. I've got to think for a second."

"Dorothea Jo, you wait one minute. I'm not done talking."

Dorothea bit her lip as she sat up and crossed her legs. "I know, Mom. But I'm too tired to think."

"If you think you're tired now, just wait until you realize the full responsibility of taking care of this baby. It's a bad idea. You can't—"

"I love you, Mom," Dorothea whispered.

"I love you, too, but—"

Though she knew it'd earn her a lecture at a later date, Dorothea hung up the phone. Lethargically, she stared at the egg for a few minutes before she gathered it into her arms. It fit snugly in her lap, and the feeling made her bottom lip quiver.

"I don't want to mess you up," she whispered. She embraced the egg, doubling over as if she intended to protect the little one from the world, whatever that entailed. "I only want to do what's best for you. But I don't know what that *is*."

Outside, raindrops spattered against the diagonal muntin windows, while inside, Dorothea's tears dripped onto the egg.

～～～

The phone rang, the pot boiled over, the baby screamed, and Dorothea tried to assuage all three with only two hands.

She'd picked up a wraparound baby carrier at a second-hand store yesterday for this exact reason. But even with the wrap secured snugly against her chest, she still needed help. She cradled the newborn's head with one hand, grabbed the corded phone from the wall—tucking it between her shoulder and chin—and then stirred the bubbling pot with her free hand.

"Hello?" Dorothea asked breathlessly before she turned to the infant, who was barely three days old. "Shh. *Shh.*"

"I see you haven't taken my advice." Dorothea's mother sniffed. "Are you at your wit's end yet?"

Dorothea bounced the baby with a few gentle shushes. Across the countertop, she caught a glimpse of herself in the wall mirror in the family room. Her hair was pulled back in a loose ponytail, but several pieces had escaped to give her a frazzled appearance. Her slate-blue pinafore—wildly out of date for everyone who didn't share her taste in vintage style—hung limp and wrinkled, bunched together by the carrier.

How laughable—was she at her wit's end? "Not yet, Mom." Although the *true* answer was *yes and no, all the time and never,* and *send help but let me do this on my own,* Dorothea replied with the *correct* answer.

"Well, you will be. Without a husband there to support you, you're going to be doing it all on your own."

The words thudded onto Dorothea's shoulders like bricks. She sagged under their weight and had to prop her hip against the oven to keep from melting to the floor. "I can do it."

A sigh. "You're such a stubborn girl. But once you stop thinking of yourself and start thinking of what's best for that child, you'll realize what you need to do. Either get married or give it a chance to have a better life than you can provide."

"She's not an *it*," Dorothea said. With the food sufficiently stirred, she flipped off the burner, placed her ladle on a dish towel, and gently moved her finger into the baby's mouth. The baby started to suck, which Dorothea took to mean that the little girl was hungry, too. Dorothea had formula and a bottle around here somewhere . . .

"Well, you didn't even tell me if it's a boy or a girl. How was I supposed to know?"

"Sorry." Dorothea switched the phone to her other shoulder and tried not to get tangled in the wire. "She's a girl. And she's got a name, too." Dorothea swallowed, hesitant to open her mouth. With every detail she divulged, she felt more and more like a little girl sharing a school project with her mother and desperately wanting praise.

Giving her any information could end badly, Dorothea's pessimistic side insisted. *Don't tell her. When has telling her anything ever worked out for you before?* But the optimistic part whispered, *She hasn't always reacted badly. This could be one of those times. This could be a good interaction. Don't be scared.*

Dorothea took a deep breath. "Augustine Rose. I call her Aggie, though."

"Well, that's cute," her mother stated in an off-handed tone.

Dorothea let out a deep, quiet breath, a smile curving her lips. At least a half-hearted reply wasn't a lecture—

"But you really shouldn't have named her. Now you're going to get attached, and it'll be so much harder to give her up when the time comes. And you *should* give her to a different family. A more well-equipped one. For her sake."

Dorothea's spirit crashed and shattered against the floor. "Oh. Well, um, I have to go. Dinner is on the stove. Love you, Mom. Tell Dad I said hi."

"I love you, too." A pause. "I only try to help because I care about you. You understand, right?"

Dorothea swallowed, unable to stave off the tears that rolled down her cheeks. But she fought to keep the emotion out of her voice, lest there be questions she couldn't answer and an interrogation that would last hours she couldn't afford to spend. "I know. Thanks."

"You're welcome."

Dorothea didn't speak again until she heard the click of the phone and felt the certainty that she was alone again in her cottage.

Almost alone.

She took Aggie out of the carrier and patted the newborn's bottom. A thick layer of blue-green hair brushed against Dorothea's cheek. Somehow, it felt like the roll of the ocean, even though it was dry. It was the most unique, special thing Dorothea had ever seen in the world, but also the reason she'd not yet been able to take Aggie out and about. She doubted everyone would find the little girl's peculiarities as precious as she did, and then the *questions*. She'd avoided calling anyone but her mother and had taken the next two weeks off work just so she could try to figure out what to do.

Numb, she hung up the phone and sank to the gray linoleum. Leaning her head against the exposed brickwork on the wall, Dorothea stared off into the distance, Aggie heavy on her chest. "I don't understand her, baby. She tells me I can't love anyone because I've never wanted to marry someone, but then she tells me not to get attached. I tell her I love her and she believes me today, but sometimes she asks me if I really love her at all. I don't *understand*. What am I supposed to do?"

Dorothea inhaled deeply, though her chest shuddered until more sobs exploded out of her. Aggie must have taken that as an invitation to join in, because she started to squall, her misery a harmony to Dorothea's.

"Oh, no. No, no. I'm sorry. I didn't mean to upset you more." Dorothea sniffed, scrubbing at her eyes. "I'm fine. It's okay. Everything will be all right."

She wondered then if she'd ever spewed a more rapid-fire series of lies in her life.

Aggie whimpered, and her eyes churned like storm clouds, the surefire threat of crankiness. But, oh. They were so pretty.

Dorothea brushed her thumb against the baby's cheek. Webbed fingers curled around one of Dorothea's knuckles; webbed toes flexed in midair. "Shh. It's okay, Aggie. It's okay. Mom . . ." Dorothea paused. Maybe she shouldn't claim the title. Her own mother's words rang in her head, reminding her of how everything could go wrong. How incapable she was of loving someone, of caring for them unselfishly. Maybe it was rude of Dorothea to ignore the fact that Aggie's biological mother was out there, right now, unable to take care of her.

But something small in her soul, something that flickered softly like the stars as they reflected on the sea, whispered to do what she felt best.

Dorothea kissed the blue-green waves of Aggie's hair and murmured, "It's okay. Mama's here. Don't cry."

Aggie didn't stop wailing, but it didn't matter. That small *something* in Dorothea's soul ignited like a tiny ember of hope.

She pressed her lips against Aggie's temple again. There—the bottle and formula rested on the table across the room.

"It's okay," Dorothea repeated. "Mama's gonna take care of you."

～〰～

Light music drifted around the coffee shop. The bell above the door tinkled as another customer entered, probably seeking refuge from the blustery late-September day. A few orange and red leaves drifted in on the wind, too, and littered the front end of the cafe. It might have been a scene worthy of an artist's illustration, except Dorothea sat like a tired lump at a table and ruined the whole ambiance. Tendrils of steam wafted from her untouched tea as she stared mutely into the caramel-colored liquid. Her fingers tightened on the cup as though she could absorb some of its warmth and apply it as a salve to her numb body.

She'd been such an idiot. Did she really think visiting her parents, sharing her deepest secret, would end happily? But after a month, she'd thought maybe, *maybe* she could risk a visit. Tell them about Aggie's true heritage now that Dorothea herself had processed it and was ready to share.

You trying to raise a regular baby is bad enough—but what is that creature? This isn't a baby; it's a monster!

Her mother's voice rang through Dorothea's mind. She might have gotten lost in the incessant clatter inside her head forever if one of Aggie's squeals hadn't distracted her.

Dorothea glanced at the car seat in the chair to her right. Aggie's mittened hands struggled to push her wool hat off her head, but she lacked several core muscles and the coordination to succeed.

"I know, baby. I know. Shh." Dorothea tugged the hat lower to ensure it covered Aggie's beautiful hair, those unique waves that had been an object of scorn two hours ago.

Tears pricked at Dorothea's eyes. How could she ever teach a child that she was beautiful, that she had nothing to hide, if she *did* have to hide? How could Dorothea teach a young, impressionable girl the difference between hiding for safety and hiding due to insecurity? If her own would-be grandparents couldn't accept her, who would? And how—

A million other worries crowded her thoughts, so loud that she didn't know how to process them all. Emotions and logistics swarmed her. She'd used all her PTO and sick days to be with Aggie the first month, and now her only hope of a babysitter had fallen through. Who else could she trust to watch a *mermaid*? And if Dorothea got permission from her boss to bring Aggie to work, mittens and a hat could only disguise her during the winter months. Come summer, she'd have to find some other way to hide Aggie's more unusual qualities.

But work wasn't even the biggest of her worries. On the worst days, when she wanted a break or just a few extra hours of sleep or a *moment* of quiet, sometimes she found herself missing the life she'd had a month ago. A selfish, horrible thought that only seemed to reinforce every doubt Dorothea's mother had sown.

Dorothea rested her forehead on the heel of her palm, her wet, tired eyes on Aggie. "I'm not a good mother, am I? I'm not prepared. And I'd rather give you up to the land pod next year than do some irreparable harm to you because I can't love anyone but myself. I want to give you the best life, even if I'm not in it." She traced a knuckle over Aggie's soft skin, which was so smooth and perfect. It'd been at least ten minutes since that plump little cheek had been kissed, so Dorothea dropped another peck there. Aggie gurgled in response.

"Sweet girl." Dorothea offered Aggie a watery half-smile. But the weight of the day forced Dorothea's head against the table, though she kept one finger in the baby carrier so Aggie could claim it.

"You all right?" A somewhat familiar voice cut into Dorothea's musings, and she jerked upright.

"Yes! Sorry. I'm fine. Sorry." Dorothea sniffed and blotted her nose with the sleeve of her cardigan. Saoirse, the barista who usually waited on Dorothea, stood at the end of the four-piece table. Since the coffee shop was only a few blocks from Dorothea's house, she dropped in for a beverage several times a week. The two had chatted frequently during these visits, as they were about the same age.

"I was just about to clock in when I saw you over here." Saoirse didn't mention Dorothea's tears, nor the red, puffy eyes and blotchy skin. "I have a few minutes to spare, so I thought I'd come over and see how everything was. You haven't stopped by the cafe in a while."

"Yeah. I'm fine," Dorothea repeated. She subtly removed her finger from Aggie's grip and pulled the canopy further over the baby. "There's been a lot going on lately."

Saoirse inclined her head toward the car seat. "You babysitting?"

Dorothea swallowed. Her tears burned her throat, which was already raw and sore. "No. She's mine." At least temporarily. "She was born last month."

"*Well.*" Saoirse blinked and claimed the seat across from Dorothea. "That means she's close in age to my youngest son! I don't know if you remember, but he's six months old now." Saoirse leaned in closer. She smelled like wildflowers and honey, and a tiny bee tattoo peeked out from underneath her black shirt collar. This close, without a bar to separate the two girls, warmth seemed to radiate from Saoirse, bringing memories of summer and sunshine that cut through the dismal fog that clung to Dorothea's mind. "I didn't even know you were pregnant. I could have given you some of my old maternity clothes." Her gaze, gentle and concerned, met Dorothea's, and she rested a hand against Dorothea's shoulder.

"Thanks, but, um, it wasn't like that. She's adopted. It was a rather . . . unexpected situation, actually." Saiorse's hands were unusually warm, and a few of the knots in Dorothea's back started to loosen.

"Oh, I see." Saiorse's eyes softened. "Are you okay?"

The sunshine-and-flowers smell seemed to weave its way into Dorothea's soul, as if searching for the winter chill that lingered in her heart. The warmth somehow made a crack in Dorothea's spirit, deep enough for all her worries to gush out of her like a river thawing from a deep freeze. "No. I'm not okay, not at all."

And for the next few minutes, everything except Aggie's heritage spilled out: the sudden adoption, the stress, the pressure, the overwhelming feeling of sinking beneath the waves of both inward and societal pressure. Things that weren't even limited to the baby leaked out, with faint hints at her failed—or perhaps unwanted—love life and her struggles with her mother's words of *too selfish to love.*

"She always thinks I'm doing the wrong thing, but especially now," Dorothea concluded. Sometime during the rush of words, she'd started crying again. "And I—I'm scared, because I think I *do* love Aggie more than anything, but sometimes I wonder if my mother *is* right. That I'll lose interest when things get too hard because I only like the rush of beginning things and can't persevere. And that I'll fail because I can't raise a kid on my own."

The edges of Saoirse's dark eyes crinkled as she squeezed Dorothea's shoulder. "And what makes you think you have to do it all on your own?"

"Because I can't get married." Dorothea groaned, dropping her head into her hands. She pressed the heels of her palms into her eyes to ward off the tears and burgeoning headache. Beside her, Aggie gurgled, unaware of the turmoil in the room. "I can't force myself to be with someone I don't love. It's not fair to them and it's not fair to me."

"Well, obviously." Saoirse snorted. "Honey. Look at me." With one hand, she gently lifted Dorothea's chin. "I'm married and have two boys of my own. My husband doesn't fix everything for me. Sometimes we need to ask for outside help, too. Because it's *okay*. You don't have to be completely self-sufficient as an adult. Anyone who tells you differently either has their own issues or is trying to control you, to make you fear you can't do anything until you can do *everything*."

Dorothea's throat clogged with emotion, and she couldn't respond to the sweet words. The scents of tea, sunshine, and lavender was almost overwhelming, but in a good way. In a calming, happy way.

"You don't have to prove anything to people who really matter." Saoirse rested her hand over Dorothea's. "You do what you can. We all do. If you need help, you ask, and the right people won't fault you or think worse of you." She smiled. "So, how can I help you today?"

〜✖〜

Sunshine soaked Dorothea as she lounged on the sand. The waves lapped against the shore, and if she didn't have so much on her mind, she might have imagined she was with the March sisters in *Little Women*, enjoying a seaside jaunt.

But her mother's age-old words churned in Dorothea's mind, still potent even though Dorothea hadn't talked to her in a few months. *Are you going to do what's right for the baby, or are you going to do what* you *want to do?*

Beside Dorothea, seven-month-old Aggie sat on her beach blanket and chewed on a teething ring shaped like a starfish. Saiorse had provided the ring, along with a basket of toys, waving away any of Dorothea's offers to pay.

"Every child needs a fairy godmother," Saiorse claimed. "It was about time I chose my godchild." And she'd patted Aggie's ocean-colored, rippling hair without flinching. Fairies, mermaids—Saoirse spoke and acted like the existence of either one didn't surprise her. No, she treated them all like everyday occurrences, and she, her husband, and their children had become the second family Dorothea needed, babysitting while Dorothea worked, hosting dinners, and filling Dorothea's life with more laughter than she thought possible.

And now, an integral part of that new life would be taken away. It felt like Beth's death in *Little Women*, the world marked distinctly in "before" and "after" the loss.

The May sun burned bright overhead as Aggie lost interest in the starfish. Instead, she smacked the sand with her tiny fist and giggled. Every sleepless night, every joy-filled morning, every tear, every laugh . . . had culminated in this.

Today, the land pod would return—and with it, Aggie's best chance . . . at least in the opinion of Dorothea's mother. A land pod would have multiple parents looking out for Aggie, after all.

And Dorothea's soul wept fiercely. As if it was determined to join Aggie in the sea one day, even if Dorothea was only a puddle of sea foam when the reunion happened.

Squirming on her tummy, Aggie paddled her legs in the air. Her shrieks of delight grew even louder when the water lapped against her tiny fingers.

Dorothea sprawled out on her stomach too, determined to see the world from her baby's eyes. The ocean seemed even better from here:

more wild, more mysterious, more all-encompassing. It called for her to dip her fingers into the waves, to be a part of something much more ancient and expansive than herself. The thought brought a smile to her face as the chilly air tickled her.

"Thank you for showing me beauty, Aggie." Dorothea dropped a kiss on the baby's bucket hat. "For letting me see life through your eyes, even for a short time."

The sting in her heart deepened.

Let her go, something that sounded like Dorothea's mother whispered. *Don't become too dependent on her, because then you're only thinking of yourself. Don't become overly attached.*

You'll never do this right. You're too selfish, Dorothea Jo.

Tears stung her eyes, and she barely had time to wipe them away before she heard footsteps and chatter to the left. Turning over, she saw a cluster of girls traipsing across the sand, led by an older woman with black-and-gray hair gathered in a braid.

It's time, part of Dorothea said, while the other part of her was too busy screaming internally to even formulate a coherent thought.

The gaggle of girls paused when they got close to the beach towel, and the woman knelt beside Aggie. "Oh? Who's this?" Behind her, the mermaids whispered and shifted. "Did we have a late hatcher last year?" the woman asked.

A few of the girls scooted in closer. Each of them resembled Aggie, with hair that tumbled down past their shoulders and eyes the ever-shifting colors of water. Some of the older girls, the ones who looked closer to eighteen, appeared even more ethereal than Aggie.

"Yes." Dorothea's voice cracked as she picked Aggie up from the sand. The baby squealed angrily until Dorothea found her pacifier. Even then, Aggie still gave unamused grunts. "Her egg got cracked, so she came too early."

"Sometimes it happens. If you're here, though, does that mean you want the baby to be raised by the land pod?" The woman herself appeared human enough. The laugh lines around her eyes were deep, and even now, she wore a soft smile that, though beautiful, had no ethereal glow. "There's no shame. More often than not, I raise most of the mers. I know parenting them can be difficult work."

Dorothea couldn't agree. Her tongue felt too big for her mouth; her neck felt too frozen to nod. But if she *had* been able to force a word out past the lump in her throat, she would have said Aggie wasn't a burden. Not in the least. She was the best blessing Dorothea could have asked for, the reason for the best and hardest and most rewarding seven months in Dorothea's relatively short life.

Selfish. Only thinking of your gain. Give the child up, Dorothea. This woman knows what she's doing. Aggie will be among her own kind. She won't need you or Saoirse or whatever makeshift family you've tried to cobble together for a poor little mermaid.

Dorothea could hear nothing else, just the inner monologue that sounded exactly like her mother. Why did she need to call home when her mother's voice never left her head?

"I just want what's best for her," Dorothea whispered, her voice so thick and quiet she almost didn't hear herself.

The older woman nodded. "I understand." Somehow, she managed to pry Aggie out of Dorothea's arms. Part of Dorothea resisted—her heart cried out for one last hug, one last kiss, for *her* to be there for the nightmares and the bad days and the temper tantrums. To help Aggie grow up fulfilled and loved and cared for, to see her precious soul bloom.

But instead, Dorothea crossed her arms over her chest so she wouldn't be tempted to reach out for Aggie one last time. She shivered inside her cardigan, the same one she'd worn on the day she'd been entrusted with Aggie's egg. Even though the May sun was hotter than the atmospheric autumn fog, Dorothea needed it for comfort today.

"Come along, girls. We'll go swimming," the woman said, turning to face her wards. Aggie's tiny face peeked over the woman's shoulder. The baby's eyes were the color of gray, cloudy skies, as if a hurricane brewed inside her tiny mind.

A look Dorothea knew all too well.

Aggie's pacifier dropped to the sand as she let out an ear-piercing cry. Like a merciless tsunami, the noise crushed the dam Dorothea had tried so hard to build in her own soul. All the tears the dam had contained burst forth in one great explosion, the poor onlookers caught in her deluge.

Both Dorothea and Aggie's sobs came in ragged heaves, but somehow, Dorothea crossed the minuscule distance to her baby in three steps. "Shh, love. Shh. It's okay. It's okay. This nice woman is going to take care of you. She knows exactly what you need." Dorothea wanted to run her fingers through Aggie's blue-green locks, which churned in unruly waves, but some force held her back. So she crossed her arms over her chest again, her heart breaking.

The woman laughed.

Dorothea blinked, and a few droplets broke free onto her cheeks. "What?"

The woman turned her head so that Dorothea could view her profile. "It's just—I don't know *exactly* what each child needs. No one can possibly know that. Each girl here is different. Eleanor wants to be alone and yells for more privacy, while Helena would be mad if I didn't press her for every little thought and emotion in her head." One of the younger girls ducked her head, her cheeks red, and an older girl giggled and nudged the one beside her. "Just because a child is a mermaid doesn't mean she is any less unique. I don't take these girls in because I know what to do. I do it because thirty years ago, my daughter was given to me when no one else wanted her." The woman rubbed Aggie's back as the baby continued to squall and stretch a chubby hand toward Dorothea. "And now I have so many daughters—and even some granddaughters." She nodded to a toddler, a child so small she had to be held by another girl. "That's my granddaughter, right there. Zelda."

"But—someone didn't teach you, or . . ." Dorothea's voice trailed off. "You didn't just miraculously know what to do?"

"Who told you being a parent is miraculously knowing just what to do?" The woman clucked her tongue. "Ask any one of these girls. I make mistakes, and I've been raising mer for thirty years. I listen. I adjust. I guide. That's all I can do."

Dorothea sniffed. "But . . . how do you know if you're ready? How do you know if you're the best person for the job?"

The woman turned and adjusted Aggie so the three of them were face to face. "You listen. There is no *ready*. But if you want to do the right thing, then that's the first step. And I think she seems very attached to you." The land pod leader bounced Aggie a few times. "I'm no expert by any means, but I think separation would devastate you both."

Though her arms were still crossed, some magnetic pull urged Dorothea to touch her baby, and Dorothea found herself reaching for Aggie. But before she could make contact, her hands faltered. "I just—I don't want to ruin her with my selfishness. I don't . . . I don't know if I can love her as much as I want to. I don't know if I'm capable."

"What utter ridiculousness. Dear, I think you're more than capable of loving this baby—and loving her well."

The statement crested over Dorothea and almost swept her feet out from under her. "What? How . . . You don't know me. You can't possibly think that."

Aggie squirmed in the woman's arms. Though she couldn't yet form any words, she babbled, a very angry tone that Dorothea recognized. It was a tone usually reserved for when a bottle or a toy wasn't immediately forthcoming.

"Dear, you can't fake the level of care I've seen from you in the last few minutes. I can see the love for this baby in your questions, your worry, your movements, your eyes. So long as you care this much, no matter what happens, I think this little one will forgive your mistakes. Look—she wants you, right now, and that's the most telling sign of all." Gently, the woman passed Aggie back to Dorothea. "You care enough to want to be the best version of yourself for her, and you're willing to sacrifice everything for her betterment. What other definition of *love* do you know?"

In Dorothea's arms, Aggie snuggled against her chest. The baby sniffled a few times and glared up at Dorothea as if to say, "*How*

*could you ever let anyone else hold me? This transgression will not easily
be forgotten."*

Dorothea laughed and offered the child her finger. With a gurgle,
Aggie stuck the pinkie into her mouth, and somehow, Dorothea knew
all would be forgiven. Especially when Aggie cooed and the storm in
her eyes lightened.

"Do *you* think you love her?" the woman asked.

Dorothea stared down at the infant. Aggie wasn't perfect; neither
was Dorothea. The days they'd spent together were exhausting—yet
filled with more sunshine than ever before.

Perhaps nothing worth doing was ever really easy. Perhaps perfection
didn't have anything to do with money, marital status, or paltry excuses.
Maybe true perfection—as close as humans could get, anyway—was
simply a willingness to do your best and learn from your mistakes. And
as for love . . .

"I love her more than anything," Dorothea whispered. "More than
I ever thought I'd love someone."

Aggie sneezed, and drool exploded all over Dorothea's hand.

Even that didn't stop the warm, fuzzy feeling currently lifting
Dorothea's spirits.

"I think you'll be just fine, then." The woman smiled before she
turned back to her children. "Come on, girls." With a few blown
kisses and calls of "goodbye," the group drifted off, a happy—if
unusual—family.

Meanwhile, in Dorothea's arms, Aggie twitched, wiping at her
nose and sniffling. Dorothea dropped a kiss onto the baby's head. "It's
okay." She lingered in the smell of saltwater that enveloped the two of
them, and for once, when she opened her heart, she didn't hear her
own mother's voice in the background.

"Mama's right here." The waves crashed beside them, and the sun
shone brightly, burning away the last of the clouds. Aggie sneezed
again, but this time, she giggled. The beautiful noise brought a smile
to Dorothea's face. "Mama will always be right here."

ACKNOWLEDGMENTS

The funny thing about books is that they aren't made just by an author. Though I put in a lot of sleepless nights, tears, and long hours, I must thank the team behind me who made it all possible. It's my name on the cover, but they had a huge hand in making this book happen.

To Anne—thank you for being such a fabulous publisher. You gave this book a home and believed in me. Thank you for your edits, for the long phone chats, and for being, above all, one of my best friends in the world. I love you so much, and you'll never know how much your friendship means to me. You are my wee little planet.

To Mariella—thank you for being such an honest editor, but most importantly, my "mom." You are such a supportive and caring friend, always checking in and sending so much love my way. You are fabulous, hilarious, and I love you beyond measure. I want to make it my life mission to show you as much care as you show me. Thanks for being such a Soft But Salty Girl™.

To Beka—thank you for being such an encouraging editor, but most importantly, my Baby Gorl. You are my Bucket Buddy, my Gus, my fellow harem sister. Thank you for being a safe place for all my emotions, secrets, and breakdowns. Without you there to keep me glued together some nights, I honestly don't know if this book would have ever come to fruition. Never doubt how much you have impacted my life. You are such a precious soul, and I love you more than words can express.

To Paden—thank you for all your wonderful ideas while I was brainstorming the short story collection. Sure, I didn't end up using any of them, but they were really, really good. Maybe someday I'll write a mermaid statue book, in case you think I forgot. Thank you for always making me laugh and being the best (and brattiest) roommate I could ask for. RIP Mr. Sizzles.

To the rest of my writing gang—Cass, Kayla, Maseeha, and Xanna. I adore each and every one of you and love you more than the world. You girls are the best. I love our long phone chats/video calls/meme exchanges. Thanks to each of you for being you.

To Mom and Dad—if I thank you in each of my books, does this mean one day I'll be your favorite kid? Because I'd like to point out that this is now my third novel in which I have you in the acknowledgments, and I don't see your names in Caleb's album liners. Also remember that I found Rosie the day she escaped, luring her back into her cage with "hamster finding music." That in itself deserves favorite child status, remember?

Above all, to God. I *know* that this book wouldn't have been made without His inspiration. I cannot thank Him enough for His mercies every day.

- Hannah

ABOUT THE AUTHOR

Hannah Carter is just a girl who still wakes up every day hoping to figure out she's secretly a mermaid. Along with *Saltwater Souls*, Hannah has also written *The Atlantis Trilogy* (published through SnowRidge Press), which contains even more mermaids, magic, and murder. Her short stories and award-winning flash fiction pieces have been published in various anthologies, including all of Twenty Hills's. She has also won Editor's Choice Award from Havok Publishing twice, for her pieces in the *Prismatic* and *World Tour* anthologies. In 2022, her flash fiction piece, "A Home for Nova," won a Realm Award. Hannah also won a competition with her short story, "Lara." In addition to fiction, she also has had over a dozen devotionals published in various magazines, as well as six devotions published in *Finding God in Anime*. In her spare time, she's probably either cuddling her cats, drinking tea, reading, or practicing for her imaginary Broadway debut. Connect with her on Instagram at @mermaidhannahwrites.

If You Enjoyed *Saltwater Souls*,
Check Out These Other Books
By Twenty Hills Publishing

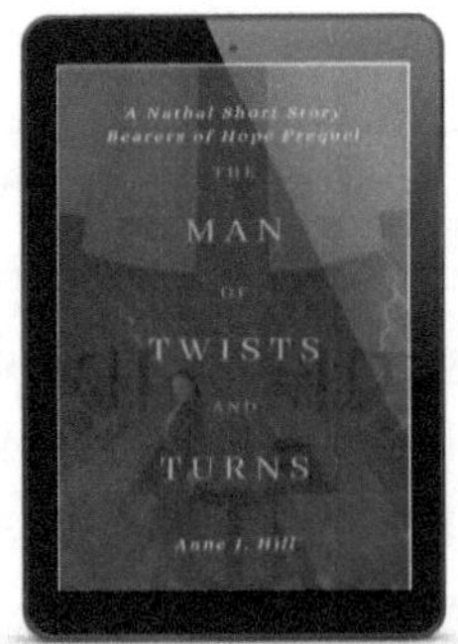

LOST NAMES

HANNAH CARTER

Once upon a time, someone asked the question: what's in a name?

And I know the answer.

Everything.

And nothing.

For you see, in the past, I have gone by many names. Each name was nothing more than a mask I wore to suit whatever purpose I had.

To inspire fear, I used the name Baba Yaga, among others. Fear has always been such a good motivator for humans. At every bump in the night, they were willing to give me whatever I wanted to appease me.

Sometimes, though, I needed to use finesse. Outwit them. Charm them, even. Because when humans feel they have risen above such a primitive, base emotion as fear—well, someone needs to remind them that there is *much* more to fear than just fear itself. Someone more intelligent than them. Someone more powerful than them.

And so, I used the name of the Pied Piper to get what I wanted. I could trick them and disappear into the annals of their history, a name with no face. A threat that became a legend.

And still, I am the winner.

But the citizens of London grew complacent. They believed that all the old threats and fears their ancestors harbored had disappeared with the turn of the twentieth century.

It was my job to remind them that they were arrogant fools.

But I had one setback since my last name had been stolen from me: the lack of a human host. In my true form, I was nothing more than the dark shadow of a wolf, a herald of winter, of cold and hunger, but unable to impact the world as I could as Baba Yaga or the Pied Piper. Without a name, without a body, mothers and fathers could soothe their children after nightmares, tell them that I could not hurt them.

A snowflake escaped from my mouth and froze a weed that dared to poke its green head out of the dark London streets. Yes, let the children believe the sweet lies that I was nothing more than the monster under the bed—it made it much easier to possess them and use them as my human hosts.

I slipped through the winding London streets in darkness. All sorts of emotions drifted on the night air to guide me. Oh, so many tantalizing ones. Wrath. Betrayal. Sorrow. Fear. They would certainly sustain me, but I grew tired of their dry taste on my tongue.

A sweeter smell ensorcelled me, much more poignant and flavorful than any of those. Yes, I could bend all the other emotions to my will, but it was too simple.

I smelled a prey much more satisfying.

Loneliness.

It drifted most potently from a two-story house.

I slithered up the ivy-covered stone wall to the open window. A young boy, barely out of his first decade, sat cross-legged on the floor. Tears stained his cheeks, and he sniffed as he trailed his hand below his nose. He clutched a pirate figurine with a missing hand.

The house was silent, save for sniffles and the loud *tick-tock* of a clock downstairs.

And then my voice.

"Home alone, child?" My voice was soft, soothing—no need to inspire fear or coerce this one. Lonely ones responded best to a listening ear.

The boy in the green shirt nodded. His eyes widened as he caught a glimpse of me on the floor. "Mmhmm." He shivered as a trail of frost formed behind me.

"Where are your parents?"

The boy stroked the wooden face of the sword-wielding swashbuckler. "I don't know. Out. Always are."

I murmured in sympathy. "Poor thing. If only you had some friends that might keep you company." I tasted vague impressions of his memories through his emotions. "But your schoolmates . . ."

The boy's face crumpled, though he didn't dissolve into hysterics. Neither did he have any words, but unbridled loneliness rolled off him in droves. So saccharine and potent—like chocolate that melted in your mouth.

"No schoolmates, either?" Emotions are so delicious, so mouth-watering, so *telling*.

"I'm better by myself," he finally said.

Delectable resignation. So young, and yet, so broken. Life had stolen this boy's light before he could even reach puberty.

I loved it.

"Are you?" The candlelight flickered as I spoke, and I grew and shrank in its glow. "Tell me, boy. If you could have anything, what would you want?"

The boy tucked his knees up to his chin. Hope flickered across his face before he squashed it—such a good little trinket. Already, half of my battle was over. Someone who had learned that hope only leads to disappointment was ready to lap up all my machinations.

"Nothing," he whispered.

"Really? Nothing?" I circled him. His eyes followed my movements, but he didn't shudder. The lonely subconscious is open to any hint of fellowship, no matter how odd. "Not even a friend?"

"No." The boy shook his head. "No friends." But he tilted his head and stared down at the painted face of his plaything. "Maybe more toys. More pirates. Maybe a crocodile for them to fight!"

Excitement crossed his face.

"Toys are safe," I agreed. I could sound congenial when I desired. "They can't hurt you. They can't leave."

The boy considered my words. Digested them. Inclined his auburn head. "Yes."

"But . . ." My promise lingered in front of him. "What if I told you I could find you friends that would never leave?"

His face darkened, and a wave of anger rolled off him, so potent—a three-course meal for me. I greedily slurped it up.

"Then you'd be a liar. Because anybody who says they'll never leave is lying." The poor boy gripped the trinket in his hand so tightly that I thought the head might pop off. "I know. Even Nanny Trudy grew up and got married and left me."

I circled him—a vulture surveying its prey—careful not to touch the pirate. I was unsure if the sword was made from iron or silver, and the latter made me wary. "But I can make you a deal. I can give you friends that will never leave you. Never grow up. Never abandon you. What do you say?"

The boy shook his head.

Ah, how pure it is to cling to innocent heartbreak instead of the promise of hope.

I heard the front door open.

"I'll come back," I assured him. "Don't worry. *I* will never abandon you."

And I kept my promise. Whatever names one might call me, one cannot deny that I was an honest creature when it suited my needs.

After all, did I or did I not get rid of those rats, just like the beggars of Hamelin asked me to?

Night after night, promise after promise, I filled that poor boy's lonely nights. I delivered toys and goodies, spun stories to elicit more emotions.

"You know," I began on one such night. "I know a place where no one *ever* grows up. We could go there."

"We could?" The boy shivered.

"We could. And we could bring as many people as you want." I rustled his figurines that were set up in line. "And have adventures. With mermaids, fairies, pirates—*friends*."

The boy swallowed. A tear slipped down his cheek until it froze from my breath.

Then he uttered the words I needed to hear: "All right. I want you to take me there—and give me friends that will *never* leave."

I licked my fangs as if I could already taste the first meal I'd have once I merged my shadow with this boy's, took over his husk, and inhabited his mind through that dark connection.

"No matter the cost?" I whispered in the darkness.

"No matter the cost."

Keep an eye out for Hannah Carter's upcoming short story collection, which features Lost Names *as well as other brand-new Nightmare Hunter stories. Publishing through Twenty Hills Publishing.*

www.annejhill.com/twenty-hills-publishing
Instagram @twenty_hills